DESTROYER

DESTROYER

THE BAD COMPANY™ BOOK FIVE

CRAIG MARTELLE

MICHAEL ANDERLE

We can't write without those who support us
On the home front, we thank you for being there for us

*We wouldn't be able to do this for a living if it weren't for our
readers*
We thank you for reading our books

DESTROYER TEAM

Thanks to our Beta Readers

Micky Cocker, Dr. Jim Caplan, Kelly O'Donnell, and John Ashmore

Thanks to the JIT Readers

John Ashmore
Jeff Eaton
James Caplan
Micky Cocker
Diane L. Smith
Kelly O'Donnell
Daniel Weigert
Dorothy Lloyd
Peter Manis
Jeff Goode
Misty Roa
Paul Westman
Thomas Ogden

If I've missed anyone, please let me know!

Editor
Lynne Stiegler

World's Worst Day Ever (WWDE)

WWDE + 20 years, Terry Henry returns from self-imposed exile. The Terry Henry Walton Chronicles detail his adventures from that time to WWDE+150

WWDE + 150 years – Michael returns to Earth. BA returns to Earth. TH & Char go to space

Key Players

- Terry Henry Walton (was forty-five on the WWDE)—called TH by his friends. Enhanced with nanocytes by Bethany Anne herself (Queen of High Tortuga after Federation is formed and Empire is dissolved), wears the rank of colonel, led the Force de Guerre (FDG), a military unit that he established on WWDE+20 years, and now leads the Bad Company's Direct Action Branch.
- Charumati (was sixty-five on the WWDE)—A

werewolf, married to Terry, carries the rank of major but is his equal partner

- Kimber (born WWDE+15 years, adopted approximately WWDE+25 years by TH & Char, enhanced on WWDE+65 years)—Major
- Her husband Auburn Weathers (enhanced on WWDE+82 years)—provides logistics support
- Kaeden (born WWDE+16 years, adopted approximately WWDE+24 years by TH & Char, enhanced on WWDE+65 years) – a major
- His wife Marcie Spires (born on WWDE+22 years, naturally enhanced)—Colonel
- Cory (born WWDE+25 years, naturally enhanced, gifted with the power to heal)
- Her husband Ramses—Major, died on Benitus Seven, WWDE+153 years
- Kailin, Auburn & Kimber's son (born on WWDE+78 years)

Vampires

- Joseph (born three hundred years before the WWDE)
- Petricia (born WWDE+30 years)

Pricolici (Werewolves that walk upright)

- Nathan Lowell (President of the Bad Company and Bethany Anne's Chief of Intelligence)
- Ecaterina (Nathan's spouse)
- Christina (Nathan & Ecaterina's daughter)

Werewolves

- Sue & Timmons (long-term members of Char's pack)
- Shonna & Merrit (long-term members of Char's pack)
- Ted (with Felicity, an enhanced human)

Weretigers born before the WWDE:

- Aaron & Yanmei

Humans (enhanced)

- Micky San Marino, Captain of the *War Axe*
- Commander Suresha, *War Axe* Department Head – Engines
- Commander MacEachthighearna (Mac), *War Axe* Department Head—Environmental
- Commander Blagun Lagunov, *War Axe* Department—Structure
- Commander Oscar Wirth, *War Axe* Department Head—Stores
- Lieutenant Clodagh Shortall, *War Axe* engine technician
- Sergeant Fitzroy, a martial arts expert and platoon sergeant
- Kelly, Capples, Fleeter, Praeter, & Duncan—mech drivers

Other Key Characters

- Dokken (a sentient German Shepherd)
- Floyd (a sentient and sweet wombat who gives gifts of poop cubes when she loves you)
- The Good King Wenceslaus (an orange tabby who thinks he's a weretiger, all fifteen pounds of him)
- K'Thrall—a Yollin, used to be systems analyst on the *War Axe*, a warrior with the Bad Company
- Clifton—human pilot of the *War Axe*
- Bundin—a four-legged shell-backed blue stalk-headed alien from Poddern
- Ankh'Po'Turn—a small bald humanoid from Crenellia. Erasmus, one of Plato's Stepchildren, is his AI
- General Smedley Butler – EI/AI on the *War Axe*, who they call The General
- Plato – Ted's AI from R&D
- Dionysus – the AI tasked to assist with running Keeg Station
- Paithoon – A Belzonian, escort for Kaeden & Marcie
- Bon Tap – a teal-skinned, silver-haired Malatian, a warrior in the Bad Company
- Slikira – an Ixtali, four legs, a spider race, called "Slicker," a warrior in the Bad Company
- Other Bad Company warriors: Tim, "Skates" Mardigan, Chris Bo Runner (Harborian), Jones, Einar, Gefelton, Eldis (wife is Xianna, a green-skinned alien woman), B'Ichi Aharche (Keome)

CHAPTER ONE

Void Space near Keeg Station, in the Dren Cluster

The alien studied the main viewscreen. A space station and a nearby shipyard. A hundred spaceships.

"We have found the infestation," the ship's commander declared.

"Lord Mantis, they have the ability to establish stable wormholes. They can travel across the galaxy in an eye-blink," a lanky alien remarked.

Dark-green skin, with two legs and three arms, a round head on a long neck with a single multi-faceted eye over a heavily fanged mouth, and nasal slits to the side of its cheeks. Membranes beside the eye vibrated as sounds fed the auditory nerve.

"We must have it," the commander replied simply. "Engage the shield."

The ship hummed for a moment and then disappeared. To those inside, it looked as if the hull were gone and they could look directly into space. From the outside, no one would know the ship was there.

"Four years we traveled to confirm what we suspected. We've been invaded."

"Aliens." The second creature placed two of his hands within a sphere and manipulated the controls of his station. "Thrust pods engaged."

"Time to target?" the commander asked.

"Six days to weapons range, Lord Mantis."

The ship's commander leaned against his station rail and studied the small image on the screen. The details would be clear soon enough. He was charged with purging the infestation. Their slow travel had created an unanticipated issue. Who would have known the aliens could build such a substantial community in so short a time?

Because they could use the wormholes. The Myriador had the shield, but they didn't have the drive. With both, the one-eyed green species would be invincible. A new plan was forming in the lord's mind.

***

"What was that bullshit?" Colonel Terry Henry Walton wasn't pleased. His face contorted and a guttural sound manifested deep within his throat. He jammed his fists against his hips and glared until the warriors looked away. "You fucking know better!"

"Yes, sir," Bon Tap shouted, a lone voice in the crowd. His fabulous silver mane flowed as the Malatian looked left, then right, for support. "You jagoffs."

He preferred human terms to those from his home planet since they were too mild for the company he kept. The Bad Company.

Slikira vibrated and made sounds that the translators didn't interpret as language. Terry studied her, trying to determine if the Ixtali was laughing or those were her natural noises. He hadn't spent much time with the spider-like race. He decided to let it go.

"One more time, and don't make me throw you into position. This isn't rocket science!" More snickers. Terry knew they were doing well, but he wanted them to do better.

The warriors moved into a small-unit staggered-line formation. They practiced in their shipsuits in the hangar bay the Bad Company's conflict resolution branch used while training on board the growing space station complex. This squad was special, made up almost completely of aliens to provide the widest variety of innate skills. An Ixtali, a Malatian, a Yollin, a Harborian, a Podder, and a Keome.

From operating in space without a suit to working in the raging heat or extreme cold, underwater to working in small ducts, they were ideal when mission conditions were ill-defined. Their skill sets were broad. Most were technicians of one sort or another, besides being some of the most effective warriors Terry Henry Walton had ever trained.

"Haven't they done enough?" Cordelia whispered to her father while he talked to himself, critiquing the unit's movements.

"They haven't gotten it exactly right. Not yet, anyway," the colonel replied.

"It's breakfast time," she clarified in a louder voice.

"It's what? Where in the hell did dinner go?" TH looked

confused, then waved his hand as if a bee were buzzing about his head. "Last run."

"Deploy," Bundin's voice boomed from the vocalization device installed beneath his shell.

Three warriors dove to the right and staggered their positions while increasing the distance between themselves. Bon Tap, Slikira, and the Harborian Chris Bo Runner shot to the left, mirroring the actions of Bundin, K'Thrall the Yollin, and B'Ichi Aharche the Keome. Their weapons pointed outboard, covering nearly three-hundred and sixty degrees.

"Target, nine o'clock," Terry shouted. The left flank of the formation dropped and aimed their shoulder-fired railguns at a distinct point. The right flank fanned out farther, crouching and drawing figure eights with the ends of their weapons as they sought pretend targets.

"Target, twelve o'clock!"

Bon Tap and Bundin swung in their original direction of travel, finding a point at which to aim.

"Fire!" The left flank bolted forward, and the right flank swung into covering positions. Bundin ambled ahead slowly but surely while Bon Tap raced into the fray, his weapon held and aimed while running. He continued to swing the barrel in conjunction with his eyes, able to fire the instant he acquired a target. Bundin's tentacle-like arms swung two pistols across a broad engagement sector. The Podder's four eyes gave him an uncanny ability to fire with deadly accuracy.

"Incoming!" Terry bellowed through hands cupped around his mouth.

Bon Tap dropped and slammed into the deck. Terry

winced at the sound of the impact. The others hit the deck with equal alacrity, if not quite the same zeal.

"Hold!" TH clapped. Cory clapped along with him while hurrying to Bon Tap to make sure he was all right. "Finally, you showed those evil Gorn who was boss."

"Gorn?" Bundin wondered. "I don't know this race, but I will research it as soon as we return to quarters."

"No need," Terry explained. "I made it up. That's more like it. Remember this, and we'll hit it tomorrow again to reinforce tactical movements. I'm told that it's breakfast time, so turn out, turn to, turn over, and take the rest of today off. Corporal Bundin, take charge of the squad and carry out the plan for the day."

Bundin waved his tentacles to bring the squad to him so he could issue orders for when they were to be back in formation.

"Seven in the morning tomorrow, right here. Dismissed," he boomed.

"You could have done that, Dad," Cory mumbled. Bon Tap ran off before she could check him over.

"But then I would usurp the small unit leader's author-ity," he stated matter-of-factly, as if reading from a manual.

He wrapped an arm protectively over her shoulders.

"Breakfast?" he asked.

"Please, no more Moonstokle Pie. That stuff is hideous."

TH recoiled in mock horror. "My own flesh and blood, turning on me."

"Appropriately so, when you have such lack of respect for your body." Cory stopped to look up at her father. "Why wasn't Mom here for this?"

"She's been trying to call Kaeden and Marcie but having no luck. Felicity is worried, too."

"They're off doing their own thing with the new Force de Guerre. 'Bringing peace on a planetary level.' Isn't that how they couched it? They'll be fine. I'm not sure I want to go out and visit them, though. Large-scale land-air battles launched from space? Who would consider that a calling?"

"Stretching their legs and doing right by the galaxy. I always expect to see them when I turn around. I miss them, too," Terry admitted.

"I miss Ramses," Cory said softly. "But I'm getting on. I don't need you to worry about me as well. I'll be right here, doing everything I can to keep others I care about from departing this existence."

TH nodded, the lump in his throat preventing him from speaking. He pulled his daughter close for a hug. They stood that way until Terry could say the words, "Sounds like it's time for an omelet with cheese and bistok."

* * *

Kimber looked across the mess hall table, glaring with increasing intensity. Sue and Timmons stared back, unswayed by her attempt at intimidation. Joseph and Petricia watched intently.

Auburn put his hand gently on Kim's leg and squeezed.

"I can do this all day," Timmons taunted.

"I got nowhere else to be," Kimber replied.

Kailin turned to Christina with an exaggerated eye roll. She snickered and shook her head.

Kim's hand shot out to push her red checker into an empty space and was withdrawing when Timmons' meaty man-paw slammed down on her fingers. She continued pulling, finally yanking them away.

"Your move," she declared as if nothing had happened. Timmons hand-lanced forward, only his index finger extended to push his piece. Kimber rolled her withdrawal into a counterswing, catching his coiled fingers under her fist. She felt and heard the crunch as at least one finger broke under her assault. He grunted and removed his hand from the board, slowly and with dignity.

"Your move," he said, wincing as the nanocytes jumped into action repairing the bones and flesh.

Kimber studied the board. Her potential moves consisted of jumps. She would have to grab her checker and jump Timmons' and then put it into place. If his attack kept her from putting her piece into place, she'd lose the piece and her turn.

She hesitated, even though she knew the sooner she did it, the more he'd be distracted by his injury. She lunged to the right as if diving away from the game, while her left hand acted as if it were independent, grabbing the checker in a no-look jump. Timmons wasn't fooled. He karate-chopped her fingers using his uninjured hand. The piece went spinning away, and Kim threw her hand up in disgust.

Timmons never pulled his hand back. He took his piece and executed a double jump before Kim could react. It was like catching the snitch.

The werewolf threw his arms in the air and stood up

from the chow hall table. "The undisputed combat checker champion!" he howled.

Timmons waggled his formerly broken fingers to make sure he was back up to full speed. Kimber crossed her arms and groaned.

"You gave it—" Auburn started.

Kimber turned to glare. "Don't you dare say, 'your best.' I lost!"

"Ever since Kae left, you've become a bit competitive." Auburn wanted to bring the issue into the open. He wanted the Kimber of old back.

"Do you like my haircut?" she asked.

"Whoa! That escalated quickly." Auburn held his hands out in front of him as he pushed his chair backward.

"I don't understand," Kailin asked Christina. She smiled at him.

"So young, and so naïve." She patted the top of his head.

"I must have been absent that day." Kai scowled and pushed Christina's hand away.

"Does this shipsuit make me look fat?" Christina asked him, pulling his chin around with a finger until he looked at her.

"You look amazingly beautiful." He beamed.

"You didn't answer my question!" She pounced. "It does. I've let myself go, and you hate me."

He recoiled in horror, and she started to laugh.

"You about gave me heart failure. Of course, it doesn't make you look fat. Why can't you say what you really mean?"

"So naïve," Kimber said. Auburn blew out the breath he'd been holding, happy to be out of the limelight.

The comm crackled to life. It didn't have to sound like that since it was efficient without background noise or wired interference, but Colonel Terry Henry Walton had asked Smedley to include it for old time's sake. The AI had quipped about TH showing his age, but everyone seemed to like it as a heads-up that a message was inbound. The mess deck instantly quieted so everyone could hear.

"TH is on his way back to the ship," Char reported. The system crackled again to suggest that was the end of the transmission.

"That's it?" Kai asked.

"She's mad at him," Kim told him nonchalantly.

"Oh, yeah," Sue agreed. "That's our cue. We better catch that shuttle back to the station."

Timmons stood and offered his hand to help Sue up.

"How are your brains wired?" Kai wondered aloud, pushing away from the table so he could take in the crowd. "TH is on his way back. It's a trivial thing, but something to be aware of."

Kimber shook her head impatiently, ticking the numbers off on her fingers as she spoke. "One. He was supposed to be back last night. Two. She never makes an announcement regarding his coming and going since they do it all the time. Three. No emotion in her voice."

"That says it all." Christina shrugged as if it were as obvious as the nose on her face.

"No emotion means Grandma's angry now." Kai threw his hands up in surrender.

"Of course, when taken in conjunction with the other two points." Kimber fixed her son with a hard look. He stared blankly back at her, a look she'd seen too often during his formative years.

"What do you think will happen when he gets back?" Kai asked.

"I don't know. We'll probably get a new assignment. It's been too long, and I'm getting antsy."

"Me, too," Christina said. "Let's see what's up. Maybe we'll have something juicy like a war over fruity drinks on a pleasure planet."

Kai grinned broadly at Christina's wink. They stood together and held hands as they headed toward the hangar deck.

CHAPTER TWO

The Myriador destroyer crept closer, slowing as it reached the limits of sensor range. "Anything?"

"No, Lord Mantis. There is no indication that these creatures are aware of our presence."

"Full stop," the commander ordered. The crew complied instantly and without question.

The ship's commander studied the sensor feedback, letting the system cycle a third and fourth time before continuing.

"Ahead point two percent light speed." The ship's maximum speed was fifty percent, but it took months to reach it, and then months to slow down from it. The lord lusted over a Gate drive, a system that would replace their backward technology.

But they had the cloak, and were invisible to the alien invaders. They had rudimentary yet effective weapons, and they weren't afraid to use them. To the contrary—Mantis relished the opportunity. Only three times previously in the history of the Myriador had an alien invasion been detected, but those had been nothing like this. Single ships attempting to colonize inner systems of the Dren Cluster had been dealt with, further reinforcing the Myriador's xenophobia. No alien could stand before them.

Mantis wouldn't be the commander who let his people down, even though this infestation was orders of magnitude more complex."

"To be the greatest, one must rise to the greatest challenge," he mused. "Take us into the enemy fleet. Prepare to drop mines."

The station's shuttle maneuvered slowly into the hangar bay, guided by Smedley's steady AI hand. Cory was first out, followed by Terry Henry Walton. Sue and Timmons held up their hands and slapped high fives on their way into the vehicle for return to Spires Harbor. No one said anything. Terry realized how tired he was after running drills for nearly twenty-four hours straight. Cory didn't look much better.

Char stood in the doorway that led into the *War Axe*. Her arms were crossed, and she impatiently tapped a foot.

TH smiled at her. "You know me..." he started, but she cut him off by tipping her head and looking out from under darkened brows.

"Shoe shopping on Onyx Station," Char declared.

"Done!" Terry said happily, stopping when Char started to shake her head.

"Complete honeymoon package."

"I like the sound of that." He sidled in and slid his arm around her waist. Peering into her eyes, he realized that wasn't all of it.

"For Cory and me to enjoy some alone time."

He deflated, the final nail hammered into his joy coffin.

"Fine. I'll work extra at the bar. It'll be one big party while you're gone, but don't think about that."

Char smiled and leaned in and kissed him. "We won't." Her eyes continued to sparkle.

"Did you tell him?" Cory asked, leaning around her father to see her mother.

Char nodded and winked.

Cory started to laugh, understanding the subtle word jousting that had taken place. Her parents knew the end result before saying their first words, but they continued the back-and-forth, each giving in their own way, never letting the magic of play fade from their relationship.

Even after a hundred and fifty years.

"Welcome back, Colonel Walton," General Smedley Butler, the ship's AI greeted TH, interrupting the family reunion. "Do you have a new mission for us?"

"I'll review the RFPs (Requests For Proposals) after I've had a shower and some chow and gotten some shut-eye." Hand in hand, Terry and Char headed up the stairs and deeper into the *War Axe*.

Cory had never understood her father's fanatical devotion to the language of his distant past. He refused to give up his roots. Her mother had left her short stint in the Navy far behind. One would never know that she had served, but the Marines had left an indelible mark on Terry Henry Walton.

It had served him well, and would again.

"What the hell happened?" Merrit shouted from the warship-turned-operations center for Spires Harbor, the fastest-growing shipyard in the entire galaxy. Vented atmosphere and internal materials created an expanding cloud at the edge of the fleet. "What ship was that?"

"Frigate 471," Ben In Ralls, the Harborian manning the console replied. His fingers flew across the panel as he sought more information. "The ship simply exploded."

"Ships don't explode for no reason," Shonna, the other half of the werewolf pair tasked with running the shipyard, noted. "Personnel on board?"

"None," Ben replied instantly.

"Replay video, expand and enhance."

"On the main screen," Dionysus replied. The AI, who was normally tasked with running Keeg Station, was assisting Spires Harbor until an appropriate artificial intelligence could be convinced that it was not beneath it to run a shipyard.

Shonna and Merrit moved closer to the screen and stared at it. Merrit pointed, and Shonna nodded. "Replay at one-tenth normal speed," Merrit ordered.

The frames flowed slowly past. "Mark one," Merrit noted. The video continued. "Mark two. Replay from twenty frames prior to mark one to mark two, and slow to two percent of normal."

Shonna pointed at the location where the explosion

started. They watched it tear into the ship, and then secondary explosions blew the ship apart.

"Dionysus, did you see what we saw?"

"An explosion from the outside in."

"Exactly. What would do that?"

"I'm sorry, Merrit. Insufficient data."

"Prepare a Pod, please. We're going out there to take a look and collect material samples for analysis," Merrit replied.

The commander didn't smile. "One down, more than a hundred to go," he stated clinically. "Prepare magnetic grapples for the remaining stock of mines. We'll deploy them directly onto the enemy ships."

"Yes, my lord." The weapons specialist tapped the order into his console and leaned back, refusing to meet his commander's gaze. There were fewer mines than enemy ships.

"Show the pattern onscreen," the commander ordered.

Instantly, the deployed mines appeared as a grid. The gaps were wider than the commander was comfortable with, but there were too many intruders, and space was immense.

"Target these vessels here and here." The commander pointed to ships at the edge of the pattern. The destroyed enemy ship had accidentally contacted the far edge of the Myriador minefield.

"The aliens have deployed a small ship to examine the wreckage," the ship's pilot reported.

"It changes nothing, except to compress our timeline. Make sure your people are working as expeditiously as possible. No breaks or meals until the grapples are ready. We'll begin phase two within two hours. Make sure the mines are ready."

The weapons specialist stood up from his position, saluted, and hurried from the bridge. There was no choice but to be ready to deploy on the commander's order.

***

"These are some bullshit jobs, Nathan," Terry told the comm screen.

The leader of the Bad Company shrugged. "Success gets you either more work or less. In this case, you are a victim of your own success, in that the systems would rather work out their issues themselves since Bad Company isn't your usual work-for-hire military team. You resolve the problem, and as often as not, it's the group that hired you that's the problem."

"They hire us for our brains as much as for our brawn." Terry leaned back and blew out a breath. He didn't have anything else to say. "I can't take any of these. These are petty squabbles for which they offer to pay next to nothing. Looks like the Bad Company will sit idle until something better comes along. Do we need to make a video or something?"

"A video? What the hell are you talking about?"

"Advertising. We need paying customers. Isn't that what companies do when looking for customers? I find it appalling that I have to advertise for my All Guns Blazing franchise, but I do. Word of mouth should be enough, but it's not. Aren't we in that same place?"

"No," Nathan replied without further explanation.

Terry waited. Nathan waited better. Terry finally caved.

"Do I have to take one of these jobs?"

Nathan snickered. "You do not. I don't want the Bad Company to be relegated to insignificance through minor actions that imply you're no better than cheap mercenaries."

"You could have started with that," Terry replied, making a face at the screen.

"I only wanted to ensure that we're on the same page. I knew we would be. What I'm working on behind the scenes is a deal with Lance Reynolds for the Bad Company's Direct Action Branch to become more of a strike team for the Federation. They have work that needs to be done, but the official capacity versus unofficial is yet to be worked out. Funding isn't a problem since the Federation's economic engine is revving at high speed."

"Money is good, Nathan, but I don't really care about that except in how it allows us to keep doing what we're doing. I've always wanted to make a difference for the better."

"I know, TH. You're a rare soul, and we don't want to burn you out or let you think you've been dumped on the trash heap of history." Nathan rubbed his chin in thought.

Even a man like Colonel Terry Henry Walton needed the respect of people *he* respected. He didn't want to live within the echo chamber of his own mind. He trusted Char's counsel, but she was on the inside with him. They didn't see what Nathan Lowell saw. They didn't have the big picture. Very few people did.

"I appreciate that, Nathan."

"Keep training, and I think we'll have some better options for you soon."

"I'll have Smedley send the rejections to these. I think we'll have a bistok roast in celebration." Terry waved and stood.

"Whoa!" Nathan exclaimed.

TH quickly sat when he realized he wasn't wearing pants. He had put on his uniform shirt for the call, expecting it to be quick and thinking they'd disconnect before either went their merry way.

"I don't know what to say," Terry said to the screen, face turning red around the perpetual stubble of his beard.

Nathan stared at the screen until his image faded to black. "Smedley! Make sure we're disconnected and send rejections to all the RFPs in the queue."

"Yes, Colonel Walton. You are disconnected. There is one RFP you have not yet reviewed. Do you want me to send the reject notice to that one, too?"

"I'll take a look first. You never know if there is a gem hidden within." Terry had started to stand, but sat back down and accessed the queue to bring up the latest request. "Holy shit!"

"Are the Harborian ships that weak?" Merrit asked.

Shonna groaned at the size of the expanding debris field. The small pieces radiated outward, and very few of the remains were recognizable. Merrit shook his head. "One explosion and the ship was vaporized."

"More or less." Shonna, an engineer by trade, didn't understand how the redundancies and bulkheads had not isolated the explosion, limiting it to the section where it had started. She leaned toward the Pod's viewscreen and asked the bits and pieces, "What happened to you?"

"I wish it was that easy," Merrit told her. "Scanning for the computer core to see if it knows more than we do, but I don't have high hopes. That ship was in cool storage, floating harmlessly at the edge of the fleet, minimal station-keeping engaged. Did it float into something?"

"The only thing it could have floated into that would have done that is—" Shonna's face dropped, and her heart started to race.

"Mines," they said together.

"Dionysus, please activate the Harborian fleet and start scanning for mines in and around the ships, then expand the search to the area between the fleet and the station," Shonna ordered.

"Activating and scanning. It will take a few minutes to bring the systems online and correlate the data."

"Standing by," Shonna replied before tapping the screen of the Pod. "For now, I think running minimal power and staying exactly where we are is important."

"I couldn't agree more. We'll find the core and anything else once it's confirmed whether we're in a minefield or not."

"How in the hell could mines get deployed here? That makes no sense whatsoever. Do that many people know we're here?"

"We have a Gate now, so maybe yes?"

"But no one's come through that Gate that we don't know!" Shonna threw up her hands in frustration, then froze as if she didn't want to shake the ship.

"If it's psychological warfare, it appears that they, whoever 'they' may be, are already winning."

CHAPTER THREE

The emergency klaxons sounded on the *War Axe*. TH nearly jumped out of his skin but recovered quickly, tearing off his uniform shirt and jumping into his shipsuit, cursing how long it was taking all the while. He stuffed his feet into his boots and bolted from the room, Char holding the door as he raced through on his way to the bridge. She pounded down the corridor, close on his heels.

What's going on? Terry relayed using his internal comm chip. Confusion gripped his mind.

There's been an incident in the shipyard, Colonel. We're assuming an emergency posture as a precaution, Micky replied.

Be there in a few, Terry replied. He couldn't imagine what kind of calamity would cause the *War Axe* to go to General Quarters.

"Something happened in Spires Harbor," he told Char as they ran.

"How would that…" She let the thought drift off since she figured TH had already asked the question.

"We'll find out soon enough. The only thing I can think

of is that Ten has escaped and is trying to take over the Harborian fleet, but that makes even less sense."

"It would be alarming," Char quipped over the klaxons.

Three flights of stairs, then through the hatch to the bridge, where the crew seemed calm. Systems was heavily occupied, while Clifton casually tapped the screen at the pilot's position. TH looked up at the captain, who was sitting cross-legged in the chair on the raised dais at the back of the bridge.

Terry gestured toward Micky.

"An unmanned Harborian ship has exploded," the skipper stated, drumming his fingers on the armrest.

"They weren't built the best. I'm surprised one hasn't exploded before now. That's why we only have ten percent manned—ones that have already had their major systems upgraded to the minimum standard of not killing the crew." Terry relaxed and breathed a sigh of relief.

"Shonna and Merrit think it hit a mine."

Terry's expression turned grim and he clenched his teeth. He looked at Char, who scowled darkly. Nothing was more terrifying than getting blown up during the simple act of going from one place to another.

"When will we know for sure?" Terry asked.

"Dionysus is working on it now, using the combined fleet's assets to scan the space in and around the shipyard."

"The board is green," Smedley remarked, confirming that all hands were in their shipsuits and at their designated posts.

Terry's mind raced, and as was his way, he started to pace, moving to the front of the bridge where he had an up close and personal view of the main screen.

Char remained near the captain, checking off a mental list of where the members of her pack were. Shonna and Merrit were running the shipyard while Sue and Timmons were building the raw materials extraction team operating out of the nearby asteroid field. She wasn't sure if they had gone out that far or stopped in Spires Harbor.

Cory was back on board the *War Axe*, as were Christina, Kai, Aaron, Yanmei, Joseph, and Petricia. All accounted for.

"Please prep the Black Eagles," Micky ordered. The weretigers Aaron and Yanmei were probably already there. They'd picked up a replacement for the one Aaron had sacrificed to destroy the evil AI called Ten. He hadn't been gun-shy about returning to the cockpit. He seemed nonplussed about it, enjoying the freedom of flying in space. The replacement was an older variant of the already aged fighters.

Yanmei wouldn't let him in hers, calling it bad luck.

"Underway," Aaron reported directly to the bridge over the fighter's comm system. "Can I ask what our mission might be?"

Micky tapped the button on his console to activate the ship-wide broadcast.

"Attention all hands, this is your captain speaking." Micky took a deep breath and shaped his thoughts in the hope that he'd be informative and not alarming. "One of the unmanned ships in Spires Harbor has exploded, possibly from impacting a mine. All ships in the area are on high alert and searching. Mines are unconfirmed at this time, but better to be ready than be caught with our pants around our ankles."

"Nice visual, Skipper," Terry said, not taking his eyes off the screen. "Now we wait."

He didn't know how often he'd be forced into that very same course of action over the next day.

"The enemy fleet has gone to full alert, Lord Mantis," the pilot reported.

Tell me something I don't know, the commander thought. "When will the mines be ready?"

"The first ten have had grapples installed, Lord Mantis," the weapons specialist replied.

"Prepare to launch on my order."

The Myriador crew scrambled to move the ten mines with the magnetic grapples into the launch tube. They'd reload after the first mines were deployed. He prayed to Myr that he'd have enough time to get the next ten done, and the ten after that. If he wasn't ready to reload when the time came, he might as well climb into the tube himself.

The gods were unrelenting, as were ship's commanders, dealing with failure in the harshest way.

"Inconclusive?" Shonna blurted. "How can all that data be inconclusive?"

"Because it is," Dionysus replied. "I cannot substantiate the existence of mines. Can you recover material from the destroyed ship, specifically anything close to the first explosion?"

Merrit looked at the screen showing a massive cloud of tiny particles spreading across thousands of cubic kilometers.

"We'll do our best," he said softly. "Engage the drive and parallel the explosion's vector."

"Engaged," the Pod replied.

"I better let the fleet know," Shonna suggested, hesitating before activating the comm links to Spires Harbor and the *War Axe*. "Ships don't just blow up."

"I know. I hope we find something. This isn't a mystery I like having unsolved." The Pod started moving toward a fleeing band of bits and pieces. "My butthole is going to pucker anytime we're out here until I know for sure."

Shonna nodded. "Attention Bad Company personnel, this is Shonna and Merrit, exploring the wreckage of Frigate 471. Dionysus has not been able to reach a conclusion regarding the existence of a mine. Recommend we stand down from the emergency condition. We'll continue to gather debris for analysis."

"Fuck that," TH stated, pounding his fist into his hand. "I thought the Harborian ships weren't built well, but that one wasn't doing anything. It wouldn't just blow up. What happened?"

"I have to stand us down," Micky remarked, not answering Terry Henry's question. "All hands, stand down from General Quarters. Resume normal watch. Captain San Marino out."

Christina, can you get the unit ready for mech drills in space?

I wondered when you were going to ask.

Terry clasped his hands behind his back and studied the main viewscreen. "Smedley, please gather the Bad Company on the hangar deck. We need to run some exercises. We're going to take our armored suits into space."

"Aye, aye, Colonel," Smedley replied sharply.

"Micky, do you need us to do any work for you while we're out there?"

"We're good, TH. Don't go too far away, and keep your eyes peeled, just in case there might be an errant mine from a war long past floating around in the void of space."

"Smedley, what's the possibility that a mine followed a cargo ship through a Gate and then disengaged to float free until it hit something?"

"The probability is not zero," the AI admitted.

"Gotta love the math," Terry grumbled.

"I could have told you that," Char said as Terry approached on his way off the bridge.

"Shall we?"

"Nothing like the sweaty smell of a mech." Char led the way out.

"Don't you take care of yours?" Terry wondered.

"Mine is the swing suit. Anyone whose armor is getting repaired or having preventive maintenance done grabs mine for training."

"That isn't right."

"I'm okay with it since we only have one suit per person."

"I know that, but what isn't right is that they don't clean it out after using it. I'm going to tear someone a new asshole. My sweat is the only sweat you have to put up with!" he declared.

"Oh, really?"

"You were the one who climbed into my bed all those years ago, you and your swishy tail and blast-furnace body. Even Clyde was cool compared to you."

"Would you acclimate already?" Char told him as they walked quickly toward the stairs. "It's been forever. If you wouldn't stay out all night training, maybe you'd get used to my hotness."

"You're not going to let that go, are you?"

"Onyx Station. Spa holiday. Cory and I enjoying some downtime."

"Once we figure out what's going on here. My gut is telling me something bad is coming."

"I don't have a good feeling about this one either."

"Is that the Etheric speaking?" Terry asked.

"I don't use that enough," Char admitted. "I'll head to our quarters and the peace and quiet to see if there is anything out there."

Char dodged out of the stairwell, and Terry Henry continued toward the hangar. He wanted to talk to Joseph and Petricia. They were the most sensitive.

"The alert has been canceled," Bundin told his squad. None of them had been aware that there had been an alert in the first place. It had taken the Podder that long to get to their quarters. He had been busy mapping out the next series of exercises while the others slept.

Bon Tap ran a hand through his fantastic silver mane, and K'Thrall's mandibles clicked his displeasure.

"Why can't we hear directly from the ship?" the Yollin complained.

"Colonel's direction. It's to prepare you to take orders via the chain of command."

"But a delay like that could be deadly. Why didn't you use the internal comm?"

"Next time, I will," Bundin replied.

Bon Tap helped Slikira to her feet, her spider-eyes catching the light to create a multi-pupiled rainbow. B'Ichi appeared, wearing a heavy parka to protect against the cold of human temperatures. Chris slapped him on the back as he walked by.

"So, we missed the emergency. It's like it never happened. What next, Bundin?" he asked happily.

"We drill," the squad leader replied.

"Who would have thought that?" Chris shot back, grinning. "What was the emergency, anyway?"

"A Harborian ship exploded."

The happiness faded from Chris' face. "Anyone lost?"

"It was one of the unmanned vessels at the edge of the fleet's open-space berthing."

Chris was relieved, his concern for his fellows addressed. It was no longer important to him. "So, when's chow?"

"Now?" Slikira added hopefully. Her metabolism required a great deal of sustenance. The Yollin did, too, and he nodded in agreement.

"Now is good."

"Do you people think of nothing else?" Bundin asked,

waving his tentacle arms in dismay at the single-mindedness of his squad.

"Train hard, eat fast, and sleep when you can," Chris offered, which was part of the Bad Company's mantra. When Colonel Walton had first heard it, he'd beamed with pride and told them that he couldn't have said it better.

"Yes, yes. Go eat your breakfast," Bundin conceded. He only needed to eat once a week, so he considered the other races' proclivity towards frequent and abundant meals to be a significant shortcoming.

"Woohoo!" Bon Tap whooped, and the five squad members ran into each other as they forced their way through the door and into the hallway. They were gone without further incident.

The Podder watched the door as if they'd pile back through at any moment, having inhaled their meals. But they didn't. Running, it would take them two minutes to get to the mess deck. He'd have at least ten minutes, and maybe as many as twenty before they reappeared and were ready to take a nap.

"I shall strive to understand you," he told the emptiness, "but I fear I never will."

CHAPTER FOUR

When Terry Henry burst onto the hangar deck, he found Christina by herself where the company usually stood in formation. Terry made a beeline toward her. She smiled as he approached, and pointed toward the cargo door that led to where the mech suits were stored and maintained.

The colonel slowed and returned her smile. "Good."

"They'll be ready soon," she replied. "Are you going to suit up?"

"Damn straight. All of us."

Cory appeared, shaking her head. "Not me."

"Except Cory."

Aaron and Yanmei waved from the back of the hangar bay, and Terry reversed course and strode toward the two Black Eagles and their weretiger pilots.

"Are we going to war, Master Terry?" Aaron asked with undue formality.

"What makes you ask that?"

"Alarms and cryptic reports. Are there mines or not? Is there an enemy lurking or not? Enquiring minds want—

no, *need*—to know!" Aaron flailed his long and gangly arms for added emphasis. Yanmei shrugged off the conversation.

"I don't know, but I'm not too keen on getting caught unprepared. I want a way to fight back, just in case."

"Of course, you do," Aaron agreed. "How long are we on standby with the birds?"

"Maybe fly cover while we have the mechs outside training?"

Aaron nodded his agreement as the first mech-suited warrior clumped onto the hangar deck, followed closely by a second and third. Soon enough, forty-four warriors stood in formation. Christina hurried into the storage hold to change. Kai leaned casually in the doorway next to Cory. The last ones to join the company were the vampires, Joseph and Petricia.

Joseph waggled the mech's fingers at the group. Terry walked briskly toward them, hoping they'd be able to help Char. As for the rest of the Bad Company, Terry wanted fifty pairs of eyes outside the ship, looking for anything odd.

But all he really needed was one mind's eye searching through the Etheric to see what couldn't be seen.

TH, there's an alien ship out there, and they are hunting us, Char reported.

"Stay inside the ship!" Terry shouted as he ran for the doorway.

"Does that mean us too?" Aaron asked. Yanmei shrugged, but climbed into her Black Eagle and started running through the pre-flight checklist. Aaron followed her lead. One never knew when Terry Henry would order the unit into action.

Judging by his rapid departure, it could happen at any moment.

Lord Mantis studied the board as his ship, *Traxinstall* held its position, making itself a hole in the fabric of space. It was invisible to the point that the stars shone through. He didn't waste any thought on what he knew.

He was fully immersed in the battle to come. Too many enemies and not enough weapons. Funnel the ships into the mines and keep them guessing; maybe get their ships to shoot each other as the ghost taunted them into recklessness. Explosions with massive secondaries. That was what he needed.

Expel the aliens. Preserve the sanctity of Myr's space. For the glory of Myriador.

Grapple mines. He had fifty to deliver precisely on target. One mine, one kill.

If only... The mines had to be delivered precisely at the most vulnerable points of the enemy ships. The commander didn't know where those were, not without scanning. And he couldn't fire up the systems because they'd give his position away. Back to guessing.

"Bring me the weapons specialist," he ordered no one in particular. Two crew jumped to their feet before quickly deciding that the closest to the hatch should run.

When they were under the cloak of the shield, they avoided internal communications systems, even though sound didn't travel through the near-vacuum of space. He took no chances. He didn't fly four years to take unnecessary risks.

He had to survive the mission. The glory of Myriador was more than a pat phrase, it was an honor and a privilege that only a very few were awarded. It was so rare that they had stopped giving it to the planet's kings. The glory was reserved for those who had risked all to save all.

Mantis had positioned himself to get this mission, and it had become more than he could have hoped for. Over the next few days, he would earn the glory, or he and his crew would be dead.

He shook his head to clear it of errant thoughts. Such a descent into self-love would ensure his demise. The enemy—they had infested the Dren Cluster, and deserved to pay for their transgressions. He'd kill them all, and take their Gate drives.

He'd destroy the massive Gate standing nearby to prevent reinforcements from arriving.

The out-of-breath weapons specialist appeared, his features haggard and his fingertips bleeding from his work on the magnetic grapples. "Yes, my Lord," he said, bowing his head. Being summoned to the bridge was never a good thing.

"I need your expertise," he said softly, as if not wanting the others to hear. "We only get one shot with each of the mines. Where are the most vulnerable locations on the enemy ships?"

The weapons specialist's heart pounded with relief. He had done nothing wrong, but it took him a moment to get past that and start looking at the problem. The commander grew impatient with the delay, and the specialist decided he'd talk through the problem. "I counted at least twenty unique ship designs. They have many similarities, but key differences as well. The ship that floated into the mine impacted it toward the propulsion end, but not at the exhaust ports. I will have to assume that their fuel is stored near the engines, making their ships fallible and vulnerable. That is where we should target our mines—the space where the fuel is stored—to deliver catastrophic damage with a single explosion."

Lord Mantis stared at his weapons specialist. "I had already reached that conclusion, but the designs are unique enough that we must have a targeting solution for every ship design—all twenty of them plus the physical Gate, and that heavy bastard that looks nothing like the others."

"I will have to study the Gate more thoroughly to determine its weaknesses. It won't have propulsion and a fuel source like the ships." The specialist started inching toward his station, torn between returning to the modification work belowdecks and his new task. "I will get you the targeting solutions before we drop the first mine, Lord Mantis."

"As soon as you can." With a hand wave, the leader dismissed the specialist.

Thirteen of the mines had been reconfigured and modified, and thirty-seven remained. Katamara hoped those working on them would get them done by the time he finished pinpointing the most vulnerable points. He would make sure of it. Once the shooting started, he wouldn't be able to leave his console, and those working below would have other more compelling tasks.

They needed to finish. He manipulated the top of his

console with his middle hand, while his other two arms worked at the globe interface. Images and data appeared before him and he started his analysis, knowing that he would be mostly guessing. Not using the sensors was limiting. He started to sweat even though the bridge was kept cool to allow the technology to perform optimally.

He hoped the commander wasn't watching him. The weapons specialist didn't dare look back.

Find the weaknesses, he implored himself.

Lord Mantis immersed himself once again in the tactical map of the enemy. A massive space station. A sprawling shipyard. A Gate half a day's journey away. More than a hundred ships in and around the shipyard. Not all would be a threat.

Passive information suggested that fully half were on minimal power, unmanned and disengaged. The commander didn't believe it. He expected they could be activated and thrown into the battle on short notice. He wasn't sure they needed crew.

The aliens were more technologically advanced than the Myriador, yet it never crossed his mind to negotiate with the infiltrators. They needed to be removed, and that was final.

The Gate had to be closed. They couldn't abide any more aliens spreading the cancer.

And that one ship that stood by itself. It surged with power. Heavily armored. It wouldn't go down easily. *Kill you first or last?* he asked himself, shaping the battle in his mind, analyzing the possibilities, and calculating his best chance for success.

For the glory of Myriador.

"What to do with you, my love?" Felicity drawled as Ted stood in the doorway to her office. Her office looked toward Spires Harbor, the shipyard named in honor of her first husband. As station manager, she had the biggest office on Keeg Station. She used it to entertain those who wanted to do business with the station, now that its existence had been made public and it had been added to the trade routes.

Business was booming—so much so that she needed to expand the station. Ted wasn't happy, since he now had to contend with people who had no business knowing that the Federation had a branch of the R2D2 research facility on the station.

"Return the station to the way it was," Ted repeated for the seventh time.

Felicity made a kissy face at her husband. "That horse has left the barn, the door is closed, and the barn is burning down. The horse shall run free like the stallion he is!"

Ted looked blankly at her, then opened his mouth to make his point for the eighth time. Felicity threw her hands up in surrender, standing to saunter toward the engineering genius. She'd learned his foibles over the years, and sometimes an impasse remained an impasse, no matter how much she wanted it to be something else.

She wrapped her arms around his neck and kissed him fully and passionately. Someone nearby cleared their throat. Felicity finished when she finished, taking the time to look into Ted's eyes afterward. He looked back, and finally, his expression softened. "I'll move the lab to the *War Axe*."

"That sounds like a perfectly reasonable accommodation until they give you one of those nice ships out there. If you had one all your own, we could go on a vacation, a lover's retreat..." She let the last words dangle, but Ted's mind had already gone to a different place, one where his own ship could be outfitted to test the latest breakthroughs.

Where no one would bother him and Plato.

He smiled awkwardly before turning and walking away. Felicity accepted the smile as genuine. She didn't need to hear his words. She knew he cared about her and the children. So deeply that it had altered who he was. She smiled to herself, thinking back to the day he had accepted her marriage contract, one of convenience for both of them.

"See you soon," she whispered as she watched him walk away.

A gentle thrumming broke through her thoughts. In the outer office, a man waited impatiently, tapping his foot to not-so-coyly grab her attention.

She smiled at him, and he started to approach. She held up her hand to stop him and shook her head. "You can go away until you learn some manners. Have a little respect. Reschedule with my assistant."

Felicity stepped into her office and closed the door on his protests. By the time she made it to her desk, he had burst in behind her.

"Dionysus, send Security to my office to arrest an intruder," she said casually. The AI was always listening. Ted had insisted on that.

"Do you know who I am?" the man blustered.

"I'm sorry that you think I care who you are. Get out of my office." Felicity was done playing, and her cold voice had a sharp edge.

"We had an appointment!" the man declared. Felicity still didn't know who he was, and would confess to being mildly surprised that he hadn't enlightened her.

But she was honest in saying that she didn't really care. It was her station, and its success or failure rested solely with her. Judging by the exponential growth, she was doing just fine without Mister Blusterbottom's assistance.

Two security guards appeared and forced their way past the man to stand between him and Felicity. Harborians. New recruits, larger than the average Harborian. The station manager approved.

"I had an appointment," the man grunted before turning to leave. The guards grabbed him from behind and deftly cuffed his wrists together. "Wait a minute!"

"Decorum must be observed in all things, whoever you are. Until you decide to respect this office and abide by the rules of decent society, you'll remain in custody. Do you understand me?"

The Harborians yanked the man around to face Felicity. She wasn't smiling. She was deadly serious.

"But..." His voice faded.

"Take him away." Felicity punctuated the order with a flick of her hand. "And thank you for getting here so quickly. My safety is in your hands when such barbarians enter the gates."

"We have ordered one of our shift security personnel to remain in the outer office while you are in yours, ma'am."

"That is very kind, but you don't have to call me 'ma'am.' It makes me sound old!" she declared in her unique southern twang. Little did they know that she was upwards of two hundred years old since she still looked to be in her thirties.

Felicity sat at her desk and accessed the comm system. "Colonel Terry Henry Walton, please."

"Now's not a good time, Felicity," Terry replied. The voice was reproduced since he was using his internal comm chip, something he rarely did.

"I wanted to tell you that Ted is transferring the R2D2 research facility to the *War Axe*. He thinks the station has gotten too crowded with ne'er-do-wells."

"Not sure when he's going to be able to get over here. There's an enemy ship out here, and we can't track it. It's got some kind of cloaking system and is invisible. We're going to General Quarters, and we'll try to turn the tables, but we can't find it. We need Ted, but we can't risk him getting hurt trying to transfer him."

"You bet your ass you can't risk hurting my husband!" Felicity blurted. "A ship? I didn't hear anything about a ship."

Felicity scowled at the screen.

Terry Henry didn't reply. He was already gone.

"Dionysus, please explain what Colonel Walton was saying."

"A Harborian ship exploded a short while ago. Despite the combined scanning systems of the Bad Company fleet, I was unable to determine the cause of the explosion. Shonna and Merrit thought it might have been caused by a mine, but I could find no evidence. I do not have any other information to corroborate Colonel Walton's claims. I'm sorry, Felicity."

"Don't be sorry, Dion. I expect TH knows what he's talking about. Continue your analysis with the presumption that an enemy ship is able to defeat our systems. Coordinate with Smedley to get Ted to the *Axe*. If they want to defeat an enemy they can't see, they will need him."

"I agree with that wholeheartedly," the AI replied.

"Wholeheartedly. What a strange thing for a machine to say." Felicity walked to her window and looked out. "Who are you, and what are you doing out there?"

CHAPTER FIVE

Captain San Marino was not amused.

"How come we can't see it?" he asked.

Terry and Char stood in front of the captain's chair and tried to convince him of the danger.

"I saw wisps in the Etheric. Things that shouldn't be there."

"But is that a ship?"

"It's not something that has been here before. I'm pretty sure," Char stated.

"Good enough for me. Sound General Quarters," Micky ordered. He leaned back in his chair and interlaced his fingers in his lap "And now the big question. Can you tell us where?"

"I wish I could. Maybe if I sat with Joseph, Petricia, Aaron, Yanmei, and Christina, we'd be able to figure it out.

Terry used his comm chip to order the five to the captain's conference room. "I'll head out with the company in Christina's place after we've picked Ted up. I think we'll need him for this one."

Char wasn't sure. "He thinks he's moving his lab here. I don't think he's expecting a running gun battle."

"Who said anything about a gun battle?" Micky interjected.

"They've already blown up one ship," Terry started.

"At the edge of the fleet, one that was in mothballs. That's not my idea of a gun battle. Maybe a little terrorist action, but no one's been hurt. If they—whoever 'they' are —come after us, they'll have their hands full." Micky crossed his arms and scowled at the main viewscreen. He glanced at his board, which was still red. Not all of the crew had returned to their GQ stations and reported ready.

"Maybe you can broadcast a message in all languages on all frequencies to see if we can get them to talk before this goes too far. If they start hurting our people, we won't be able to dial it back."

Smedley replied, "Will do. Broadcasting a message of peace and goodwill."

"I doubt they'll talk to us." Micky slowly shook his head.

"I do, too, but how would we feel if we hadn't tried?"

"Like shit," Micky answered unnecessarily. "We'll keep running it until we don't need to. I expect it will be clear when we've reached that point."

Terry looked at Char one last time. She tipped her chin to him, and he nodded back. She disappeared into the captain's conference room, while Terry headed out the main hatch on his way to the hangar bay. It was time to suit up. He wanted the firepower that the mechs provided. He wasn't sure the Bad Company's Direct Action Branch could take out a spaceship with just the weapons carried by the armored suits, but that didn't mean he wasn't going to try.

Somewhere out there, a faceless enemy waited.

The weapons specialist started to sweat. The computer had efficiently helped him to map out the target locations on each of twenty-odd different enemy hull-types, including the Gate and the main space station. The bottom line was that the *Traxinstall* didn't have sufficient weaponry to destroy the enemy.

He knew the commander had come to that same conclusion.

And the magnetic grapple installation had slowed significantly with his departure. He was being set up for failure—a spectacular downfall—because he couldn't come through. He exposed the fangs encircling his rounded mouth. Once he accepted that he could not deliver what the commander wanted and that he would be summarily executed for his incompetence, better options were available.

He pulled up the tactical maps and rolled through the enemy targets. His breathing slowed as he stood. Prepared to accept his fate, he turned and faced the commander.

"Lord Mantis, I am incapable of achieving total destruction of the enemy, but if we want to drive them from the system, there may be another way." The Myriador weapons specialist stood at attention, counting his remaining life in seconds, not years.

"Finally, the truth," the commander replied. "Before we

dropped our first mine, I had already come to that conclusion. Do you think I am half-assing this?"

"Of course not, Lord Mantis!" the specialist blurted. The bridge crew was silent, trying not to be caught watching as the scene played out. The specialist didn't flinch. He lowered his voice and said firmly, "We can win this fight, for the glory of Myriador."

"Explain," Mantis commanded. His expression suggested he wanted a fresh opinion.

"We leave the Gate and drive them to it. Hit and run. Scare them into fleeing. The *Traxinstall* can destroy ten, maybe twenty ships before they hazard a guess where we are. And we hit the station when they are in disarray. We hit it hard, and then issue an ultimatum."

"You want us to talk to the aliens?" the commander replied suggestively.

"It is yet another course in a series of tactical maneuvers, Lord Mantis."

The commander motioned for the weapons specialist to join him at the three-dimensional tactical display. "My thinking was to hit them here and here," he pointed at the outer sectors of the shipyard, "to drive them toward the minefield. We need to attain a certain level of attrition in order to instill fear. Once they are properly afraid, they will bend easily to our will."

"And then we hit them along this flank, to channel them toward the Gate. Once it has been opened, we'll let as many of them as possible leave."

"But not before they evacuate their station. I doubt they would leave their people behind," the specialist answered.

"What makes you say that?"

"Because I would not. We cannot assume the aliens are less honorable than we are. If they *do* leave their people behind, we destroy the station with energy weapons. At our leisure. But if we believe that they will want to evacuate their people, then we can't let them open the Gate until the evacuation is ready. If they call for reinforcements, our mission will fail."

The commander lifted his head to look down his nose at the upstart.

"You say what we are afraid to. There is a high risk that this mission will fail." He faced the bridge crew, studiously avoiding looking at him.

"Eyeballs," he demanded, and started to pace, walking past each station as he spoke loudly in defiance of his own rule about silence. "There is also a chance that this mission will succeed. The glory of Myriador! It is what we have served our entire careers for.

"Now is the greatest chance any of us have ever had. This isn't a lone scout ship with a small crew digging in the rocks. This is a military force with a gross tonnage that exceeds the entirety of the Myriador fleet, and we are but one ship. Yes, it has been said right here on this bridge: our mission could fail. It *should* fail, but when we stand, one against many, we stand for our people and the sanctity of our space. We cannot allow this infestation to continue. For the glory of Myriador!"

———

Terry struggled into his suit, which smelled of sweat. He had only himself to blame. He should have cleaned it better after its last use. The suit powered up, welcoming him with a series of diagnostics, all resulting in green lights. He flexed the systems and reveled in the power the suit brought. He ran through his weapon systems, including hoisting the railgun, then strolled through the oversized corridors leading from the mechs' maintenance and storage space to the hangar bay.

The company was milling about, not doing anything productive.

"Capples! What the hell do you have going on here?" Terry blared over the suit's external speakers.

"Company, Fall in!" the sergeant ordered. The mechs stopped playing their various games of grab-ass and hurried into two platoons of three squads each. Kimber appeared from the shadows, with Auburn close by.

Terry clicked over to a person-to-person channel.

"We've got an enemy ship out there!" Terry started. "What the hell are you guys doing?"

"Trying to figure out what the hell is going on. No one, including you, is telling us anything!" Her retort came as a stinging rebuke. "We were digging in with Smedley to figure out what the hell is going on."

"Point taken," Terry conceded. "Form the company."

Kimber pointed at the company, which was already in formation. "Are you okay, Dad?"

Terry's eidetic memory was renowned throughout the Federation. He missed nothing, usually. He remained trusting and even naive regarding certain things, but when it came to war, he was laser-focused. A sponge for information, and a super-computer who turned that into intelligence before delivering a battle plan that had always guaranteed victory.

"I think so," he replied softly. "Maybe my brain hit max density." He made a show of shaking his head sideways as if trying to get water out of his ear.

"You should have the docs check you out."

"I *love* those guys," TH stated, sarcasm heavy with each word.

"I'm telling Mom."

"Of course, you are." Terry chuckled at the leverage his daughter used to bend him to her will. It ran through the women in his family. They all knew how to manipulate him.

Appropriately so.

"What do you say we get ready to kick some ass?"

"Just let us know what that ass looks like and where it is, maybe why it needs to be kicked, and all the information."

"Jeez! You get that knife blade into the crack so you can keep wedging it in there, twisting and turning." Terry gestured for Kimber and Auburn to lead the way. They both clumped ahead in their suits. When they were in place, Terry looked from left to right, taking in his warriors, who were identical in their heavy armor.

So much firepower. More than any regiment of Marines from his past. Inside the suits, the men and women of the Bad Company were driven, like him, like the Marines, but they didn't wear the eagle, globe, and anchor. They weren't even a formal military.

But they were his comrades in arms. He would

continue going to war with them until war was no longer needed, and then he'd fade away, as all warriors do.

Over time, because times change. Wars change. Generations embrace someone new. That day had not yet come. This was still his day.

"Bad Company," he bellowed, reveling in the sound of a military order. "At ease!"

They were in their suits, so nothing changed. With the armor on, they would have relaxed, shaken out tense muscles and turned their attention to the colonel. He couldn't see within the metal shells, so had to assume they were doing all three.

"Char has felt a disturbance in the force," he started, but no one snickered. After he said it, he didn't find it funny either. It had sounded better in his mind. "There's a cloaked ship out there, hidden from our sensors and barely recognizable through the Etheric. Whoever or whatever they are, they aren't coming forward. They don't appear to be interested in talking.

"We're broadcasting messages into the void of space, trying to get them to talk to us. The last thing we want is to engage in a fight right here. We have family and friends scattered throughout Keeg Station and Spires Harbor, and even right on this ship.

"We don't usually fight space battles in our mechs while we're out in space, but this one's different. This bastard is silent and invisible. Maybe with our Mark One eyeballs, we'll be able to see him when all the technology at our command cannot. We'll light him up, and like a beacon, that'll draw every weapon in the fleet. We've lost one ship, a Harborian frigate that was in cold storage.

"I have no intention of losing any more, not if I can help it. First order of business is to move the *War Axe* close to the station so Ted and his equipment can transfer aboard. We'll deploy like a cordon between the *Axe* and the station's hangar bay to make sure Ted makes it on board safely. Then we'll recover.

"With Ted's help, maybe we'll find this guy sooner rather than later, but we're going to be suited up for some time. If you're not ready, let me know. We have a war to fight. I can feel it in my bones. So hit the head and grab one last protein bar or whatever you need, but pretty soon, we're going to be knee-deep in the shit. I'll need you by my side and ready to fight. Company, attention! When I give the command to fall out, you'll fall out, unfuck yourselves, and within ten minutes, you'll fall back in. We'll be ready to collect Ted at that point. Fall out!"

A third of the company unsealed their suits and hopped out the back with rigid efficiency before running from the hangar bay for the head or the chow hall. Terry strolled down the line of warriors, nodding appreciatively at the unit he'd built with Bad Company funds. Kimber joined him.

"Do we know anything about the enemy ship?" she asked without preamble.

"As close to nothing as possible. All we have is a blown-up ship and a ghost in the Etheric."

"Did Shonna and Merrit find anything in the debris?" Auburn wondered.

"Massive secondaries. It was like they knew exactly where to hit us." Terry looked out the open hangar doors at the shimmering forcefield as the ship moved toward Keeg

Station. "We should probably check the outside of the ship when we stop. Take one platoon and perform a visual inspection of all the vulnerable spots, at least. I'll make sure Ted gets on board. I'm sure he's bringing all his stuff."

A large dog ran across the hangar bay, stopped in front of Terry Henry Walton, and stared at the reflective helmet shield.

Your wombat is pooping everywhere. Make it stop, Dokken said.

"How'd you know it was me?" Terry asked.

It doesn't take this fabulous nose of mine to figure out which suit you've befouled.

"Hey!" TH blurted. "You know what they say. Everyone likes a little ass, but no one likes a smart ass."

Well? Wombat?

"What happened to the cleaning bot that follows her around?"

She gave it the slip.

"That's my little girl!" Terry said proudly.

"Brother..." Kimber grumbled. Terry slapped the back of her suit with his armored hand. She heard it more than felt it.

How would you like it if I pooped everywhere? the dog asked.

"But you wouldn't."

I know. It's kind of disgusting, like those wombat cubes she insists on leaving everywhere.

The warriors started to return.

"Put Cory on it," Terry told the German Shepherd. "And you need to get out of the hangar bay in case we have an emergency decompression."

Don't you have any duct tape?

"We all do, but that's not the point. I've sworn off taping dogs to my face. You licked my mouth."

You liked it.

"I most assuredly did not!" Terry declared. He reached a metal hand down to the huge dog and scratched behind his ears. "Go on, now. We've got a fight coming up, and Cory will need you close. Take care of her for me."

You can guarantee that, Dokken replied. *But make sure your dumb ass makes it back home in one piece. Little ass, smart ass, dumb ass! Hahahahaha.*

Terry watched Dokken go. At one time, his faithful companion would have been in his own suit and at the colonel's side, but that wasn't his job anymore. He needed to be Cory's companion, and take care of her because Cory's husband, Ramses, was gone. It was a huge void, and the dog filled it as well as he could. Terry was glad.

When the warriors were suited up, Kimber directed one platoon to the side while Terry led the other platoon to the open bay door.

CHAPTER SIX

"Smedley, make sure the hangar bay is clear and prepare to decompress. First squad, take the left, second, to the right, and third on high. Form a triangle through which a shuttle will pass. Keep your eyes outboard, ladies and gentlemen. You're looking for something that is trying to hide, so anything that seems odd needs to be reported."

The squads affirmed their orders and waited.

"Hangar bay is secure. Prepare to decompress," Smedley reported before starting a ten-second countdown. The shimmer disappeared right after the air was sucked into storage for use later to restore the atmosphere.

Artificial gravity disappeared with the forcefield. The warriors remained attached to the deck. With a hand-and-arm signal, a tomahawk chop to point the direction, First Squad launched out to Terry's left. Second Squad jetted to the right, and Third Squad shot toward the ceiling before reorienting and heading into space to secure the top of Terry's triangle.

The warriors moved into position and began their visual search.

Kimber's platoon zoomed out the door and broke into teams of two, spreading into a three-hundred-and-sixty-degree pattern. The hangar bay entry was at the front of the heavily modified destroyer, so she needed her people to head out before circling back to overfly the hull, looking for that which did not belong.

Once they disappeared, Terry activated his jets and slowly spun as he flew toward the station's open hangar bay. Its forcefield would remain in place but still allow the transit of a mech and a shuttle Pod. The *War Axe* could have done that, but it was easier for his people to get in and out of an unpressurized zero-gee space.

"Cap, have someone keep an eye on the hangar bay entrance. Let's make sure our friend out there doesn't get the idea to sneak in, just in case they truly *are* invisible."

"On it, Colonel," Sergeant Capples replied before relaying the order to the last warrior of Second Squad, who moved back into the hangar bay and secured himself to the deck to maintain a vigil over the entrance. "Eldis is linked in with Smedley as a redundant measure."

"Roger," TH confirmed before continuing toward the station. He adjusted his orientation to fly through the opening feet-first and head up, landing heavily as the gravity sucked him down to the deck. He strolled to the Pod that was loading. Ted was aggravated, wildly swinging his arms and mumbling. Felicity was trying to calm him down.

"We've got beer on the ship," Terry interjected at nearly

maximum volume. The workers returned to what they were doing, and Ted threw his arms up in frustration.

"Beer?" Ted asked.

"What matters is getting you over there, where you'll be safer and able to help us find the enemy ship."

"What enemy ship? Maybe I should use *Ramses' Pride* instead," Ted turned away.

"We could use an additional asset. Bring it over. We'll park it in the hangar bay."

Ted ignored him.

Felicity answered. "It's currently broken."

"Ted's ship is broken? How did that happen?" In the back of his mind, Terry was pleased since it kept Ted as a captive audience on board the *War Axe*.

"You don't want to know," Felicity dodged.

Yes, I really do want to know, Terry thought, but he didn't verbalize it. They needed to get going. An enemy ship was out there somewhere, and as long as he was jaw-jacking, the enemy was the only one doing the hunting. The colonel preferred action to reaction. "Let's go, people. We have a job to do, and it isn't getting done while we're over here."

"The large combat vessel is indisposed," the weapons specialist stated with a dark smile, pointing at the *War Axe* as it assumed a nose-first position nearly touching the station.

"If we attack that ship, a catastrophic explosion would probably destroy the station." The commander scratched his jaw with one hand while he rubbed the other two together.

"They have people outside the ship. We could be spotted."

An enhanced image showed the mech-suited warriors drifting over the hull.

"It was a good thought while it lasted," the commander conceded. "Prepare to execute the original plan. Pilot, take us to Attack Point Angelor. Weapons, prepare to launch the first two mines and energize the plasma driver."

"Two of the mines will hit ships here and here, and we'll fire on a ship here." The weapons specialist pointed to three disparate targets, vessels that were separated far enough to give the impression of multiple attacking ships.

"Underway," the pilot reported.

The weapons specialist assumed his tactical station and immediately checked on the status of the mine reconfiguration. Not all the mines were upgraded with magnetic grapples. It would take another day to get the last ten finished once combat began since the engineers would be pulled away to other duties. He snarled at the report and shook his head to clear it. He had another battle to fight, and every shot had to count.

"Attack Point Angelor," the pilot announced.

"Launching weapon number one," the weapons specialist stated. The calculations for launch angle and speed had been taken into account, and a small pack was on board to fire, slowing the mine before it impacted the enemy ship's hull.

The first mine sailed toward the target, a cold destroyer-class ship just like the second mine target. The third would be a battleship that was powered-up and active.

The *Traxinstall* would take that one on directly. Five shots, and then reengage the shield. The plasma weapon and the shield also couldn't be used at the same time. The specialist wondered if the aliens had better power sources. They could use those as well as the Gate.

This place was like a toy store for adults. So much worth taking. The weapons specialist changed the trajectory on the second weapon to disable the destroyer. After the fleet fled in terror and the station was eliminated, they could return to a few wounded vessels and take what they wanted. Yes. That was the revised plan. His "incompetence" would be rewarded with riches beyond compare.

Until then, it would be his secret.

"Launching the second weapon," the specialist stated, and the mine proceeded exactly on its adjusted trajectory. The *Traxinstall* remained shielded. It would expose itself to the aliens at the right time, when the plasma attack began.

"Got you!" Merrit's face brightened as a critical piece from the destroyed frigate floated into the cargo space of the small shuttle. He secured the hatch, repressurized the interior, and headed into the back.

Shonna was in before him, working the piece carefully while letting the scanning systems do their job. It only took a few moments before Dionysus was able to deliver the result. "It's heavily irradiated from what is undoubtedly a miniaturized nuclear device."

"A nuke went off in our shipyard, and no one could tell until we pulled this piece in?" Merrit stared in disbelief. "That's bullshit. We have to have better sensors than that."

"The explosion occurred too close to the engine's energy system, which, when blown up, looks nearly identical. Nearly."

"You can tell this wasn't the engine?" Shonna clarified.

"It is not from the engine. This piece was irradiated in space as it was blown inward. In human parlance, you are holding the smoking gun."

"Get on the hook and let everyone know," Merrit ordered.

An explosion nearby sent a piece from another ship bouncing off the Pod's hull. Shonna and Merrit rushed back into the cockpit and studied the screen. A destroyer had been ripped apart. It was no longer recognizable, but not pulverized like the frigate had been.

The light of a mini-sun flashed from the other side, and another destroyer fractured into pieces, secondary explosions bright, until the oxygen burned off and darkness returned.

Above them, a ship materialized where they had just seen stars. A massive plasma cannon running along the lower hull erupted and sent a glowing energy ball toward a Harborian battleship. Then another and another. The barrel started to superheat.

They watched in fascination until the fifth shot, then the ship started to disappear, turning before it was invisible. Merrit slammed the engine to full and raced toward the spot where the ship had last been seen.

"Impact imminent," Dionysus stated clinically.

The Pod slammed into something they couldn't see, slewing sideways after impact and drifting with the loss of power. Somewhere behind the werewolves, atmosphere whistled as it escaped through a rupture in the hull.

"Terry Henry, Dionysus just reported that the Harborian ship was destroyed by a tactical nuclear device," Micky transmitted to Terry's armored suit.

"Get on your fucking horse and let's go!" Terry roared at Ted as he continued to delay. With care, Terry picked Ted up and tossed him through the open hatch. "Secure it and get to the *War Axe* right fucking now!"

TH pushed the shuttle as if that would hurry things along.

"I have it, Colonel. Please stand clear," Smedley remarked. The small ship lifted off the deck, rotated, and shot straight through the opening like a bullet being fired. In a matter of seconds, it pulled up and hovered, waiting for the Bad Company warriors to return.

"Return to the *War Axe*. All hands. Double-time!" Terry broadcast as he ran toward the hangar bay opening. He dove through like Superman and ignited his jets to accelerate toward his ship. "Bring it in, people."

The mini-supernovas coming from the shipyard told him everything he needed to know. He saw a strange spot of light that soon after fired plasma beams at another spot. It disappeared, and the darkness returned.

"Replay that," Terry ordered his suit. "And magnify."

A tiny ship appeared at the extreme edge of the ship's

optical capture. It was a third the size of the Harborian battleship upon which it fired, making it about half the size of the *War Axe*, and it had already killed three ships. The battleship didn't explode, but each plasma discharge was a direct hit. Without active gravitic shields, the damage would have been nearly catastrophic. The ship hadn't exploded, but it was probably dead.

He touched down inside the destroyer's hangar bay, his vision of the shipyard now blocked. All he could see was the great expanse of Keeg Station, a massive and vulnerable target.

"Felicity, you better move your people away from the outer hull. Shelter behind secondary bulkheads while we go kill this bastard. You won't be safe until he's dead."

"I understand," Felicity replied into a portable comm device. She sounded like she was running.

"Micky, my people are still outside the ship. As soon as they're back inside, button us up and establish an erratic course between the enemy and the station. We have to stay here and protect the station, as much as I want to hunt that bastard down."

"Will do, Colonel," the skipper replied with unnecessary formality. Keeg Station was a Bad Company asset, and when it came to the Dren Cluster, Colonel Terry Henry Walton was in command.

"And get the Harborian fleet moving. Those with gravitic shields, activate them and charge weapons. Shoot to kill." Terry switched channels. "Come on Kimber, pick up the pace. We have a battle to win."

"Almost there," she replied. As if to put an exclamation

point on it, two suits arced from overhead at full acceleration until they were aimed at the hangar bay.

"Squad leaders, report."

A series of "all present" replies came through, along with two reports from platoon commanders that verified all warriors were accounted for. The last two mechs through were Kimber and Auburn.

"Secure the hangar, Smedley." Terry Henry's weight settled as gravity quickly returned, and he released his boots' magnetic clamps. The forcefield shimmered into place, and air rushed back into the space. A light by the hatch leading into the ship started flashing red, then green, followed by burning a solid green.

Ted's shuttle settled, and he stormed out when the hatch opened.

"Stow it!" Terry growled. "We're under fire. If you want to save Felicity's life, you need to figure out a way to find this bastard."

"Felicity?" Ted's face screwed up with confusion. "I just left her without saying goodbye because of you."

"She's fine for now, but we're under attack. The station is the most vulnerable target, even with moving to the spindle core."

"Yes," Ted replied, relaxing. "They'll be safer there. I'll be in Combat Information. Tell them to bring my stuff."

Ted waved a hand indiscriminately toward the suited warriors.

"Third Squad. Ditch your suits right here and carry Ted's stuff to him. If we want to win, that man will give us an edge. Kimber, take charge of the mechs and keep them rotating through ready status. We won't get any warning if we need to take an in extremis action. I'll be on the bridge."

Terry parked his suit by the hatch leading to the ship's interior and carefully powered down. He climbed out the back, glancing over his shoulder to see Third Squad doing as he had done—parking their suits close to the bulkhead in an orderly fashion and climbing out. The colonel bolted through the hatch and headed up the stairs.

"I'm bringing a big bucket of 'fuck you' to pour over your head."

CHAPTER SEVEN

Terry and Micky stood side by side as they watched the replay on the main screen. "Smedley, work with Dionysus to see if there were any detectable energy surges before and after that ship's appearance. Any changes in the visible and invisible spectrums. Tell me sensor systems were active during that time."

"Shonna and Merrit were in a shuttle in close proximity to the ship when it appeared and collected a great deal of data before they lost power."

"They *what*? How did they lose power? Where are they now?" Terry rapid-fired his questions.

"I believe they rammed the enemy ship. They lost power after that."

"Who is going to get them?"

"The Harborian ships are hesitant to move because of the enemy's activity," Smedley noted.

"Tell Dionysus to take over the closest ship and go get our people!" Terry clenched his fists and tensed his jaw so hard that his cheek muscles clicked.

"*We* can't," Micky said before Terry could order the *War Axe* into action.

"I know," Terry said before relaxing. "Our primary duty is to protect the station."

"Our primary duty is to finish that alien ship. We've stopped broadcasting our message of peace, just for reference."

"You said you'd know when the time was right." Terry steepled his fingers in front of his face as he concentrated on the tactical screen. "If you were him, what would you do?"

"Kill the Gate and trap us here, unless he knows we have Gate drives, and then the Gate is irrelevant," Micky started. "Then it would be a war of attrition. He didn't attack us first when he had surprise on his side. That might have been his greatest tactical error."

"Dionysus has assumed control of a hot frigate and it is en route."

"Thanks, Smedley." TH looked at Micky and nodded for him to continue.

"He dropped mini-nukes on the destroyers, but fired up the battleship with a plasma cannon, making himself vulnerable during that brief period."

"Five rapid-fire shots. How long was he visible, three seconds?"

"Exactly three."

"That's your window, Smedley. You have that long to acquire the target and fire everything you can bring to bear."

"I shall endeavor to succeed," the AI replied.

"I have no doubt about that."

"What's his plan, Micky?"

"Destroy us one ship at a time. Divide and conquer."

"That's what I was thinking, but we're not dividing. Watch at the Harborians. They're clustering closer and tighter—those that don't look like chickens with their heads cut off."

Icons representing ships raced in erratic patterns. A light flashed, and one of the ship icons turned red. "Did the ship appear?" Terry hadn't thought that it had. "Smedley, enhance and replay live video."

The screen displayed a slightly grainy image showing the ship in question conducting a series of erratic maneuvers as if trying to stymie the enemy's aim. An explosion at the front washed over and through the shield, enveloping the ship in a brief fireball that quickly disappeared as the oxygen vented from the ship.

"It ran into something," Terry and Micky both said.

"Mark on the screen where the first explosion was, and then mark this one. Ignore the three ships lost during the active attack."

"Shonna's and Merrit's Pod has been recovered. They are alive and well."

Terry breathed a sigh of relief and smiled at the screen. "Finally, some good news. Get them on the horn as soon as you can."

Lines appeared on the screen between the first explosion and the latest.

"Are you seeing what I'm seeing?" Micky asked, drawing a line in the air with his finger. Terry nodded.

"Add in the last three attacks." They appeared on the screen. Terry rotated and twisted the tactical image using well-practiced hand gestures, exploring how it looked from all angles.

"If I didn't know better, I'd say there's only one enemy ship, and he's trying to herd us toward the Gate."

"That's what I was thinking," Micky concurred.

"Smedley, get Dionysus to fire up a few of the Harborian ships in cold storage and take them through the Gate. Give the appearance that we're conducting an evacuation."

"Will we need their firepower?" the AI asked.

"Their weapons are useless. If we can see the enemy, we can kill it all by ourselves. Those ships provide an opportunity to bring him out of hiding. Send five, is all. The rest of the ships are to bring overwhelming firepower as soon as we know where to aim." Terry crossed his arms and glared at the screen. "This isn't a stand-up fight. We won't get the chance to punch him in the mouth. He's going to slip and slide his way around Keeg Station and Spires Harbor. We'll have to pick at him like gnats until we get a good shot."

"Merrit is on the comm," Smedley announced.

"Are you guys okay?"

"We've been worse. Just a few bumps, and then there was that issue where we lost all of our air, but the shipsuits came in handy," Merrit replied.

"What did you learn about our friend?"

"They are fully invisible. We were close, like *really* close, and after they disappeared we slammed into them, so even from a range of a few meters, I saw stars where they were, but they were solid. We wrecked the Pod. It's probably not coming back from that one."

"It was solid while it was invisible?" Terry asked, keying on the one bit of news he could use.

"Hard as the Rock of Gibraltar."

"Make sure all your data gets scrubbed and shared with Ted. He's on board the *Axe* now."

"I'm sure Dionysus has already taken care of it."

"Get back to Spires Harbor and give those folks a little backbone. They're not doing me proud."

"We heard. Kill this son of a bitch, TH. He lined up and shot that battleship and then moved on. He's a heartless fuck."

"We're doing what we can." Terry signed off, knowing that he sounded weak. He felt weak, too. They couldn't see the enemy, but he could see them.

Terry gripped Micky's shoulder before leaving the bridge through the captain's conference room, where he hoped to find Char and the others. When the door slid open, he found them all head-down on the table. It looked like they were sleeping. He tiptoed next to Char and took a knee. With one finger he brushed the silver stripe of hair away from her eye.

Her lid fluttered and she looked at him dully, without her usual sparkle. "All of that to tell you nothing you don't already know," she lamented. "We could see him clearly when he appeared. Their aura was bright in the Etheric before it shrouded itself and disappeared again. It has taken all our effort to see only that."

Terry kissed her forehead softly and slowly stroked her hair. When he stood up, the others looked at him through tired eyes.

"Got any of that for me?" Joseph croaked before clearing his throat.

Terry shook his head and turned to the weretigers. "I'll need you in the Eagles as soon as you're able."

"On our way," Aaron replied, giving Terry a thumbs-up, his chin continuing to rest on the table with his arms lying like wet pasta before him.

Terry wanted to parry with a witty comeback, but nothing came to him. The others watched him expectantly, looking disappointed as the seconds ticked by.

Maybe Shakespeare. "From *Midsummer Night's Dream*: and sleep, that sometimes shuts up sorrow's eye, steal me awhile from mine own company. And my own addition to the quote, make sometime not a long time, err we lose ourselves within the dust of space."

"Touché, TH." Aaron repeated his thumbs-up.

What's wrong with my mind? Terry thought as he painted a fake smile on his face and departed, hesitant in his step since he wasn't sure. When the door closed behind him, he stopped.

"Combat Information to check in on Ted," Terry verbalized a mental checklist. "Then the hangar bay to put Kimber in charge of the operation. My place is on the bridge. A hundred ships are at my command. The chessmaster must not become a piece on the board."

"Who's bored?" Cory asked when she stepped from the stairwell into the corridor. Dokken and Floyd followed. The dog pointed with his head toward the wombat, who ran to Terry when she saw him.

Terry! she cried happily.

He picked her up and briskly petted her, stopping for a moment to feel that the ship was moving, but deliberately, not with the fury of a destroyer engaged in combat. "I hear you've been marking more territory."

Yup! For my friends.

"The whole ship is filled with your friends, so you don't need to mark, little girl. Please use the restroom like everyone else."

Not poo! Signs of my love.

"Well, *this* is what love looks like to me, and what I appreciate the most." Terry looked at Floyd's beady and dark eyes while continuing to pet her.

Me, too.

"Perfect. Please don't mark. Dokken doesn't like it. His nose is much more sensitive than ours."

Dog mean!

Terry chuckled. "Dokken isn't mean. He has his redeeming features." Terry looked at the dog, who was trying and failing to roll his eyes. "I have to go now."

He tried to hand Floyd to Cory, who crossed her arms as the wombat struggled mightily to stay in Terry's arms. Dokken sat and cocked his head sideways as if calculating odds of who would win the human-wombat skirmish.

"I'll take you with me," Terry capitulated. Cory uncrossed her arms, put her hand on her father's shoulder, and smiled. A soft blue glow appeared under her hand.

"Are you in pain?" Cory asked, suddenly concerned. She tried to look under her hand, but the shipsuit was in the way.

"I don't think so," Terry replied before trying to hurry away, unable to take his eyes off Cory's hand. He walked into the bulkhead beside the hatch, grunted, and turned to watch where he was going. He increased the length of his stride until he hit the steps, taking them two at a time on his way down to the CIC.

"I don't think so," he repeated to himself, shrugging it off. "I'm in pretty good shape for an old guy! Old Marines never die, they go to space and live on, bringing the big hammer of Justice to the galaxy."

He started to laugh, shaking off his earlier discombobulation. He jumped to the landing where he would exit the stairwell as the ship bucked from an impact to the shields.

Smedley?

The enemy ship appeared and fired a single plasma projectile at us. It disappeared as I fired. I fear that I didn't hit it.

Bracketing fire, Smedley. Assume that it is going somewhere other than where it is headed when visible, including not staying where it is. Take the shotgun-blast approach to this bastard.

I have input your direction into the targeting systems. He shall not go unscathed next time.

If there's a next time. Any damage?

None, Colonel Walton. The War Axe *is as stalwart as ever,* the AI replied.

"I would expect no less. General Smedley Butler, hero to all!" Terry declared aloud. "If he's shooting at us, he isn't shooting at anyone else."

Terry hurried to the CIC and entered to find two of the terminals dismantled and Ted sitting on the deck working with fiber interfaces.

"Can't you hold the ship still?" Ted declared in a tone that suggested it wasn't a question. He glanced at the wombat, made a face, and returned his gaze to TH.

"Not when we're under fire. You know what we need, and I have to assume you're working on it. The only question that remains is how long until we can see that ship?"

"I'm working to reconfigure our scanning systems. Once I've collected more data, I'll probably still not be able to give you an estimate. Plato?"

A new voice resounded throughout the operations space. Plato. "I've analyzed the data that Dionysus collected with Shonna and Merrit. I can tell you what doesn't work. That is the limit of what I know regarding seeing what is invisible."

"So, you don't know? We'll do it the hard way, then. Thanks for coming on board, Ted. Can I send some food or drink for you? Is there anything you need?"

"I need peace and quiet. Kill that ship so I can work on finding it without its interference." Ted laughed at his own joke and dug back into his lapful of fiber optic cables.

Terry walked away without looking back, happy that Ted was in a good mood. He absentmindedly stroked the wombat in his arms.

Now, the hard part. How do I find you?

"They are chasing their tails," the weapons specialist stated as he watched the heavy destroyer perform a series of erratic maneuvers following the attack.

"Their response was quicker than I would have thought," the commander noted.

"You knew how fast it would be, Lord Mantis. They were ready for us, yet weren't able to fire before we were gone."

"Chalk not up to skill what is solely in luck's purview," the commander quoted from the Myriador fleet's strategy and tactics manual.

"Give credit where credit is due, Lord Mantis. For the glory of Myriador."

"Indeed."

The two studied the three-dimensional tactical display.

"None have moved toward their Gate."

"I anticipated that. It would be best for them if they simply left, but they don't seem the type to give up when they have invested so much. Wait." The commander pointed to five ships that had broken away from the shipyard. The image of the Gate magnified, showing an energy signature that was at the far end of their ship's ability to measure. An event horizon replaced the stars beyond.

The five ships conducted a slow arc one after the other to align themselves with the open Gate. The first one was well ahead of the other four.

"They are afraid of mines. Go forth, aliens! Your escape door is open," the weapons specialist muttered under his breath.

After the first ship had disappeared through the Gate, the other four went through rapidly, one after the other. The Gate powered down.

"There is hope yet for their cowardice, but they left their people on the station behind."

"I've calculated that if they use half their ships, they should be able to move the combined assets in the shipyard and the station," the weapons specialist stated.

The commander studied him with a critical eye. "How did you estimate the number of aliens?"

"I used what we found on the ships at the edge of the storage area."

"Fool! Those ships were in cold storage. Our systems couldn't penetrate the station. Your guess is meaningless. Go help those idiots finish the mines."

The specialist couldn't contain his surprise and shock.

"Of course, I know. Part of being in charge is training those under your command. You are failing in that. You have presented information in a way that I find compelling, but you have failed your people. Get down there and finish that work." The commander waved his center hand angrily, shooing his subordinate away.

The weapons specialist hurried off the bridge.

"Take us to attack point, Dulisto," the commander ordered Helm.

CHAPTER EIGHT

"They left without us?" Bon Tap said, his voice a high-pitched whine.

"Our mission is to find a ship and contribute to this battle," Bundin declared.

"What's going on? What battle? The *War Axe* is still here!" K'Thrall pointed out of the hangar bay to where the heavy destroyer shot past during a series of tactical maneuvers. "Hey! They're pretty close to the station."

Bundin recounted everything he had learned from Joseph. Although they were able to talk through telepathy, the communications chip that had finally been configured for the Podder's brain made conversations quicker and more accurate. The *War Axe* was close enough that Joseph had reached out to tell his friend all he knew about the intruder.

Information was power. The others had been up to their usual antics, as Bundin had seen it, but it was their downtime that they relished. He could see how they were tightening up as a team, growing close to the point where they could anticipate each other's actions. He couldn't, but wanted to. He knew what he had to do, but being social with the aliens wasn't his thing.

As their leader, it was critical.

"We must solve this problem," he suggested.

"How to get back to the *Axe*?" Slikira asked.

Bundin's stalk head waved around while he tried to control his tentacle arms. "The bigger question is, how do we contribute to this fight?"

"With our own ship," K'Thrall offered. "Ted's ship is right there. I say we take it."

"Why didn't he take it?" Bundin countered.

Chris waved down a deckhand from the hangar crew, and they chatted briefly before Chris turned back to the squad. "It's undergoing repairs and modifications, but it's almost ready. Only a couple hours remain."

The team looked through the forcefield at the stars and the shipyard in the distance. A bright flash suggested a battle was taking place out there while the *War Axe* protected the station, using its bulk as a physical shield.

"Will the battle still be happening in two hours?" B'Ichi asked from within his well-heated suit.

"Dammit!" Terry shouted when he got the news of another explosion near the shipyard.

"I've got it," Kimber told him. "Your place is on the bridge."

She tried to shoo him away, but he hesitated. "He's out there."

"And we're going to do him, upside-down and backward. We'll find him, and you can bet, if any of these good people can, they'll rip his ship apart with their mech hands."

Terry nodded, his face a grim mask of anger and grief. At this point in the big game, they were losing. They were down five ships, with five more having gone through the Gate.

"Go!" Kimber pointed at the hatch.

Terry jogged across the hangar bay with Floyd firmly in his arms and into the ship.

"Another enemy ship has impacted a mine in the field, Lord Mantis," the pilot reported.

The commander regretted his initial strategy. Unless he pushed a mass of ships through the minefield at one time, they'd figure out where the field was, causing him to waste precious resources. He could assume they had already figured it out.

"Change of plan," he declared. "Recover the surviving deployed mines."

Delivering and recovering the mines took no extra power. They could do that with the shield securely in place, hiding the *Traxinstall* from prying eyes. They left the last attack point before firing weapons and headed to the far end of the minefield, and the crew smiled darkly as the ship flew between and past the enemy vessels, taking the shortest route to their destination.

They moved deliberately but without hurry. Their power was in their stealth.

I will kill each and every one of you, no matter how long it takes. For the glory of Myriador.

Terry rushed through the hatch and almost ran over his wife. Char looked beyond exhausted.

"Go to bed," he told her, supporting her until she collapsed. He held her with one arm and put Floyd on the deck with the other. Then, Terry picked her up in his arms and carried her, although he didn't want to leave the bridge. He turned to Micky. "Any good news, Skipper?"

"I think you were right, TH, but it'll wait if you need to go."

Terry shook his head and pointed at the main screen with his chin.

"Right." Micky didn't want to argue. "The last explosion shows what could be a double strand of mines along a single axis."

"Straight line?"

"Yes."

"What do you say we power up the mains and send a few thousand projectiles down that line? See if we can get lucky," Terry suggested.

"That would leave the station unattended," Micky countered.

"Move a couple of the Harborian battlewagons over here. We can head out as soon as they're on station. Hell, bring some frigates for escort duty. Let's camp a shitload of metal between the station and open space."

"I like that plan, as long as Dionysus or Plato is in charge of the ships. I don't trust the spacefaring skills of the Harborians. Not yet, anyway."

"I'm with you, Micky. Execute the plan. I'll be back as soon as possible." Terry went through the captain's conference room on his way off the bridge to check on the others. They had crashed where they were. Christina was on the table, sound asleep. The weretigers had made it as far as the door before they laid down on the floor. The vampires were beneath the table. Cory waved from where she sat at the table. Dokken was sitting by her side.

Floyd waddled toward her and stopped when she saw the dog. The two stared at each other.

Terry nuzzled Char's face. "I don't understand what you had to do, but I know that you gave it all you had trying to help me. To help us," he mumbled into her hair.

"I've never seen it take this much out of them," Cory said softly, patting for Floyd to jump into her lap. The wombat hesitated before running and bouncing off Dokken as she jumped. Cory caught her and held her tightly. Floyd turned around and stuck her tongue out at Dokken.

I am at a loss, he complained.

Be the bigger man, Terry told the dog. *She's just a little girl, no more than a puppy.*

I know, but can't you train her a little more quickly?

I think she is trained about all she's going to get, buddy. She'll be forever young. Maybe we should be envious of her instead of trying to change her? She might be the happiest creature I've ever met. You're a grumpy old man.

You're *the grumpy old man,* Dokken retorted before lying down, head between his paws. *I'll think about it.*

That's all I can ask. You're a good boy, Dokken, no matter how old you are.

The large German Shepherd closed his eyes and feigned sleep as Terry left the room with Char in his arms. He could feel the ship moving. He hurried toward the stairs.

"Deactivating Mine L7-16T," the weapons specialist stated evenly. Each weapon carried a unique designation and had a unique disarm code to prevent an enemy from deactivating an entire field with a single series of commands. The disarming was done in close proximity to the mine using a directed millimeter wave beam to limit the chance it would get intercepted by an enemy.

The *Traxinstall* floated serenely as the weapons specialist manipulated the digital commands, entering one after another, handshakes, verifications, more codes, and finally the beacon extinguished. "Bring it in," he ordered.

His subordinates used a remote control to drive the mine toward the launch door. There was only one tube, so during recovery operations, other mines couldn't be launched.

They'd never contemplated having to launch mines while recovering them at the same time.

"Bring it all the way in, and attach a magnetic grapple,"

he ordered. "That makes one, only a hundred and seven to go."

The commander watched from the bridge. He resisted the urge to tap his foot or drum his fingers to release the energy that was building up within him. The larger ships were starting to move. With massive weapons, it would take one direct hit to vaporize his ship.

No direct hits. Stay hidden. Stay two moves ahead. The game board was changing, and he wasn't sure what it meant. He stood to study the tactical display.

They were reinforcing the station.

Good.

It would leave him free to recover his deployed weapons and use them more intelligently.

That big bastard was moving. It headed toward deep space before approaching the end of the minefield on a direct course toward the *Traxinstall*. The commander's heart leapt into his throat. He could barely breathe. It was like they were visible.

"Verify shield status!" he demanded. "Quickly."

"Nominal, Lord Mantis," a hand at the engineering station reported.

Nominal. Operating within normal parameters.

"Prepare to move the ship," the commander said evenly as he focused like a laser on the enemy heavy destroyer.

***

Terry made it back to the bridge completely unencumbered. The wombat was with Cory, and Char was tucked in in their quarters. Terry strolled forward to look at the screen.

"Good positioning, Micky," he said, leaning down to eyeball a direct line across where the two ships had been destroyed. "Are we powered up and ready to fire?"

"We are. Care to do the honors?"

"Don't mind if I do," Terry replied. He spread his arms as if readying a prayer or a fantasy fireball. "Fire the mains."

The destroyer thrummed as the projectiles were accelerated to near light speed. Smedley adjusted the heading to create a spiral flow of lethality swinging around and through the estimated line of mines.

They were rewarded with an explosion, and far in the distance, another.

"Maintain your fire," Terry encouraged. "How many did you put out here?"

The mains took a break to cool down and then engaged at the cyclic rate of fire a second time. Something sparked in the distance, appeared for a second, and then disappeared.

"There he is! Concentrate in a circle around that location." Terry stabbed his finger at the speck in the distance. It was taking too long, two to three seconds to drag the line of fire through that position. He was too far away.

Or was he?

"Damage report!" the commander ordered.

"Shield reset and is restored. Damage to the outer hull did not breach. It was a glancing blow only."

"Minus five thousand. Get us out of here, now!"

The ship rocketed straight downward, pressing the envelope of how fast it could go and remain shielded. It started to slow as it approached the ordered distance.

"A breach in main stowage," an environmental technician reported from the side shadows of the bridge.

The commander didn't blink as he turned to face the one who had issued the report. "How bad?"

"At least fifty percent of the supplies before the emergency bulkhead activated."

Eight-year missions needed certain supplies despite the best recycling and reuse machines Myriador had to offer.

"Drop markers on those supplies," the commander ordered.

"Already done, Lord Mantis," the technician replied.

"We'll recover them after this mission is over and not before." The bridge crew kept their eyes on their stations. The commander checked the tactical display. The big ship continued to rain destruction through the minefield. Seven explosions registered the demise of mines that would never deliver a death blow to the enemies of Myriador.

"Prepare to attack the station," the commander ordered in a cold voice.

CHAPTER NINE

"The ship is ready?" Bundin asked.

"It can be flown, but this is Ted's ship," the engineer responded as he put his tools into their appropriate places in his kit.

"Dionysus, can you fly Ted's ship and take us into battle?"

"Of course, but Ted hasn't approved the use of his ship."

"I do," Felicity interjected from somewhere out of sight. "We need our Bad Company warriors out there where they can deal with the threat. Ted's ship in the hangar bay does no one any good. Launch *Ramses' Chariot* immediately."

The engineer shrugged. "Not my call." He sobered before standing and bowing his head slightly. "Good luck out there."

Bon Tap jogged by and slapped five on the engineer's outstretched hand. Chris Bo Runner did the same as they jogged aboard. The others followed. Bundin couldn't reach with his tentacle arms, so he bounced his shell off the man's hand instead as he hurried toward the ship.

"A hand, please," he said on reaching the entry ramp. He had to be turned sideways to fit through the hatch, as he had learned on his trip with Ted and Cory to Earth. The squad reached out to twist him and drag him through. He bounced his stalk head off the metal only once before he filled the corridor. The ramp withdrew and the hatch closed.

"Sorry about that," K'Thrall said, not sounding sorry at all. "To the bridge!"

The Yollin led the way to the bridge where he assumed a position near the captain's chair from which he could access the ship's systems.

"Oooh!" He purred at the expanse of sensors and equipment providing streams of data he'd never seen before. "Give me a minute."

As a four-legged Yollin, he couldn't sit in the captain's position, although he wanted to. The Podder couldn't fit on the bridge, so he waited in the corridor outside, wedged against the doorway where he could see the main screens. Bon Tap joyously bounced in, flopped into the captain's chair, and tossed his head, sending a wave through his silver mane.

B'Ichi waited in the corridor with the squad leader. "I don't like space travel," he admitted.

Bundin didn't need to turn to see the Keome since he had eyes on all sides of his head. He wouldn't have been able to turn his shell body without help anyway since he was firmly ensconced in the narrow corridor. "And you think I do?"

The Keome smiled and started to laugh; the sound registered from his heat suit as a high-to-low-pitch siren's call. "Who said the corporal didn't have a sense of humor?" He continued to laugh.

All of them had said that. Bundin joined in with a low rumble that bounced off the deck plates from beneath his shell.

Slicker worked her way onto the bridge and squeezed into the pilot's seat. "Humans," she complained.

Bon Tap snickered while Chris leaned over his shoulder and watched.

"I have to ask: what do we do now?" Chris held his hands up to emphasize his point, that being how powerless they were to do anything.

"Welcome to my nightmare!" the AI's voice boomed throughout the ship, followed by metal guitars shredding some riff. Hands shot to heads and covered ears. "Sorry about that. I don't get to play much when Sir Theodore and Plato are at the helm. Actually, I don't get to play at all. But now it's just us blue-footed boobies turned loose against our arch-enemy, the unseen."

The image of a bird appeared on the screen, a feathered creature with a bill for catching fish and extremely blue webbed feet—the blue-footed booby.

"We don't look like that," Slicker said, her eyes reeling from the image and her head still pounding from the heavy metal.

The screen adjusted to show the view in front of the *Ramses' Chariot* as it lifted off the deck, turned, and accelerated into space.

"The first order of business is to find the enemy."

The firepower of the *War Axe* burst onto the viewscreen as Dionysus enhanced the image.

"What are they shooting at? Should we go over there?" Chris asked.

"They are sweeping the minefield with their railguns, using particle acceleration to detonate the weapons in place," Dionysus replied.

"They don't seem to be hitting much," Bundin offered.

"The mines, like the enemy ship, are invisible to all systems. The *War Axe* is sweeping the area with fire."

"Should we join them?" Bon Tap wondered, reiterating Chris Bo Runner's question.

"No," K'Thrall stated definitively. "The *Chariot*'s sensors are different from anything the other ships have. I think we need to start scanning the area of the minefield for anomalies that we can use to refine our search until we can recognize a distinctive pattern from the enemy ship. Finding that ship is our number-one purpose. I suspect anyone can kill it if they know where to shoot, based on how the *War Axe* is blowing up the mines. The cloak does not protect what hides behind it, it appears."

"Concur," Dionysus stated, and slowed as it activated the myriad of systems at its command. "Scanning and parsing."

"And now we wait," K'Thrall said as another mine exploded under the *War Axe*'s onslaught.

"That's thirteen mines," the weapons specialist stated after the latest explosion.

"They'll stop firing when the station comes under attack. After that, we'll return to collecting our ordnance."

The commander stood near the tactical display, studying it. His center hand reached into the map and started high-lighting locations. "Rapid fire, one shot to each of these locations."

"Yes, Lord Mantis," the weapons specialist replied, transferring the data to his position.

"Navigation, randomly skew heading thirty degrees at each materialization point. We will not go in the direction we face until the fifth shot, after which we will return to the minefield."

The pilot accelerated the ship as the navigator detailed the movements at their shared station.

"They will suffer for their intransigence," the commander stated as the station grew larger on the main viewscreen.

The first firing position exploited a gap between two battleships and the *Traxinstall* hovered, weapons charged. "Strap in and hold on," the commander ordered. "Damage Control, prepare for action."

They hadn't stood down from their previous engage-ment. They acknowledged that they had firefighting and hull-breach repair equipment ready for action. They stood in the corridor, strapped to the bulkhead, quick-release levers in their gloved hands, their suits providing air for them to breathe and a controlled environment from which they could work within a breached section.

Although they could do so, none of them wanted to see the rest of their supplies jettisoned into space. They wouldn't survive the trip home. Some of them already doubted that they would ever leave this area. A grazing blow from a single weapon had nearly destroyed their ship.

Death was in the hands of the aliens, but the damage control team would do their duty. As would everyone on the crew.

"Fire," the commander ordered.

The shield dropped as the main plasma cannon sent its deadly stream between the monstrous alien ships. Within milliseconds after the weapon had fired, the shield rolled back into place, a blanket within which the ship could hide, but it was vulnerable. *Traxinstall* jerked sideways and headed for its second firing location, not far from the first.

Enemy fire ripped through the space where the Myriador had been.

"Direct hit," the weapons specialist declared before adding, "Plasma cannon is ready to fire."

"Fire."

The ship materialized from the void of space and fired, disappearing to race around the other side of the station. Ships moved toward it, but it was already gone. The pilot jockeyed between an aggressive frigate and a stationary battleship, smoothly accelerating away.

"Fire," the commander ordered a third time.

The weapons specialist snarled with the fury of the plasma cannon. He watched the impact when a huge part of the station ripped away after a violent secondary explosion.

The station bucked and screamed under the onslaught, but the secondary bulkheads remained stalwart, limiting the buffeting from the explosions. But the gathered group of evacuees could hear it and feel it all the way to their bones.

Felicity stood her ground, glaring at the wall as if her eyes could bore through to an enemy who would attack innocents. She clenched her fists until her nails bit into her palms, and still she squeezed.

"Kill them!" she yelled at the bulkhead. Five attacks and the explosions stopped. "Dionysus, is he gone?"

"I have no way to tell, but I am working on something. Please stand by."

"What? I'm not good with waiting, honey!" Felicity said to the bulkhead. Dionysus had already gone back to what he was working on.

"Fuck me!" Bon Tap blurted as the enemy ship appeared almost on top of them. It fired as it materialized, then disappeared before they could take their next breath.

"Tell me you got something," K'Thrall said as numbers washed across his screen. A systems analyst in a previous life, he couldn't keep up with everything Ted's ship was capable of providing. He had to count on the AI to interpolate, encapsulate, and explain.

"I can tell you what that ship is carrying in regards to weaponry and personnel. They appeared in the middle of an active scan, so I was able to collect a great deal of data in the short time they were visible."

"They stopped firing. Do you think that was something we did?" Slicker asked.

"We did nothing," Bundin replied. "I suggest that the

commander of the enemy ship is operating according to an engagement strategy that meets his objectives. We will probably never find out directly what his objectives are. We'll have to guess, based on what we can observe."

"Like the fact that he's trying to blow the shit out of the station?" Chris snarked.

"Like the fact that it appears the *War Axe* has ceased firing on the minefield and is en route to the station, where it appears our friend no longer is," Bundin posited.

"A diversion," K'Thrall muttered. "Dionysus? You have something?"

"I cannot yet track the ship, but I know that I will be able to if given enough time. The attack on the station was haphazard and impacted minimal systems. No injuries and despite appearances, there is minimal structural damage. Unfortunately, the great window of the All Guns Blazing is no more, and much of what was within was vented to space." Dionysus delivered the damage report.

"The colonel isn't going to be happy about that." K'Thrall shook his head, mandibles clicking his dismay at not being able to solve the problem of the enemy ship.

B'Ichi remained confused. Space wasn't where he wanted to spend his life, and he had little understanding of ships. None of what was happening made any sense to him.

"Why would they attack in the first place?"

"If we knew that, we could start a dialogue to resolve his concerns," Bundin answered.

"But what if his only goal is to kill us all?"

"As of right now, that is the only thing that makes sense, but he's going about it slowly and deliberately, which suggests power might be a limiting factor. He can't rain plasma into the station because he'd remain exposed too long. He's vulnerable," K'Thrall offered from his position by the scrolling system display.

"My scan of his ship revealed that there are one hundred and ten carbon-based entities, and seventy-four similar devices that I conclude are mines. He has the plasma cannon and less potent point defense weaponry. His ship was unshielded, which means that K'Thrall is correct. The enemy is extremely vulnerable. All we need to do is hit him one time, and he'll come apart catastrophically."

"We need to tell the colonel," Bundin said.

"Already done, Corporal," Dionysus replied. "I don't keep secrets."

"Good to know," Slicker interjected. "Except that one that's just between us."

"Of course," the AI replied.

K'Thrall threw himself into the data, mumbling as he tried to make heads or tails of it. Slicker leaned over and watched, her multi-faceted eyes magnifying and reflecting the streams.

Bon Tap ran his fingers through his hair. He sat in the captain's chair, but he had no idea what a real captain would do. He spun the chair to face the doorway from which the squad leader waited and watched.

"What do we do?" Bon Tap found himself asking again. He didn't want to be known as the guy without a clue, but it was rapidly becoming apparent that was exactly what he was. He stopped playing with his hair and looked for guidance.

"He's returning to the minefield," Bundin said with

certainty. "We shall join him. Dionysus, follow the alien to the minefield."

"I cannot follow what I cannot see."

"Of course, you can. The *War Axe* reported seeing the alien. Show it on the screen, please. And where the mines were destroyed. Two strings with the alien right in the middle? He's pulling up the mines. But why? A marginal attack on the station to stop the destruction of his weapons. Is he regretting laying them in the first place?"

"You need to talk to Captain San Marino and Colonel Walton. Your insight is more than any other speculation that has been relayed." Without waiting, Dionysus made the connection.

CHAPTER TEN

Terry rubbed his chin in thought as he examined the information Dionysus displayed on the *War Axe's* main screen. Bundin had made a compelling argument, and Micky had stopped the ship halfway between the minefield and the station. They held their position, with gravitic shields at full strength and the crew at combat stations.

"If he fucked up, why would he keep shooting? He could slink away, and we'd never know that he left." Terry crossed his arms and tossed his head. "What are you up to?" he asked the alien captain rhetorically.

"If he would only answer," Micky remarked.

"You're not suggesting we start our play-nice transmissions again?" Terry turned on the captain.

"No. I want him to come to us with an explanation." Micky leaned back in his chair and watched the screen. The symbols were starting to blur into each other, so he climbed down from the captain's dais. "I'm on my last reserve, TH. I'm going to catch a few zees. Call me if anything changes."

"I'll hold down the fort." Terry climbed into the captain's chair and tapped the button for the ship-wide broadcast. "Attention all hands. Fifty-percent watch. Let's get some rest, people. Hour naps in place and rotate."

"The station has just been attacked, and you're standing down?" Smedley inquired.

"Bundin has given me a good perspective on the situation, and I am convinced he's right. We have time. This bastard is going to return to the minefield to recover his mines. When we hit him, if he's loaded up, the explosion will be spectacular. Too bad we won't find a piece big enough to put in a shoe box."

"What if he redeploys those weapons?" Smedley pressed.

"Minesweepers. We will bombard the area with the full spectrum of electromagnetic waves. I think we'll find a way to detonate them. We'll flood the area with so much noise, they'll have to blow. Maybe if we blast enough debris through the area, it'll leave a hole in the cloud..."

Terry stopped talking and visualized how there would be a dead space beyond the physical object of an invisible ship. Rocks and debris instead of electromagnetic waves.

He activated his chip for a direct comm link, holding his finger to his temple as he usually did, knowing that Ted preferred the quicker communication so it wouldn't interrupt him and his train of thought.

What if we bombard the area where we think that ship is hiding? A massive debris pattern?

If you put enough debris into space, none of our other sensors will work.

How are they working now? Terry asked, not amused by Ted's answer.

Telling us nothing, Ted admitted, before continuing in a more excited tone, *Your special squad has taken my ship. They are to bring it here immediately.*

Can't you fly it?

It appears they've convinced Dionysus of the greater positive impact if the ship remains in space and trailing the enemy.

They can track the enemy? Terry stood up on the dais, hope surging through his system. *Bundin didn't say that.*

No. They have, with Dionysus' help, achieved a more accurate-than-average guess as to the enemy commander's intentions.

Terry considered the caveats that Ted included in his reply. *I'll take that as a good thing. We'll keep* Ramses' Chariot *out there trailing the enemy, but with shields in place and the Gate drive energized. They can leave before a weapon could hit them.*

They better not hurt my ship.

We're all government property, Ted. I'll tell them to do their best not to scratch the paint.

Terry sat back down and sighed. He had no intention of telling the crew of *Ramses' Chariot* to take it easy. Dionysus was flying the ship and K'Thrall and Bundin were on board, and they were warriors to whom Terry had entrusted his life. If they wrecked the ship, it would be for a good reason. He put those thoughts out of his mind.

"Smedley, make sure you stay tight with Dionysus. I want you to know everything he knows when he knows it."

"I'm not sure I can do that. His is a greater mind than mine."

"Not when it comes to fighting an enemy. How about you focus on everything he knows when it comes to our invisible enemy?"

"I can do that. I thought you said everything."

"Human version of everything," Terry corrected. He stopped to listen to the internal reporting as the crew and the warriors of the Bad Company stood watch at fifty percent. Half would be on duty while the other half rested. It wasn't optimal, but this battle would be fought minute by minute, and it could spread out over days.

His people had to be ready when the time came.

"Ruzfell," Terry called to the new systems analyst. "What will it take to send a wide debris field across a large area of space?"

"Asteroids. We can hit them with the mains once they're on course."

"Fill the hangar bay with asteroids. I like it."

The alien nodded. "Clifton, move us toward the asteroid field, and Smedley, get Timmons on the line and send the department heads to the hangar bay. I need their input to make sure this plan will work."

***

"Where are they going?" Bon Tap asked.

Slicker turned, her head shaking as she laughed.

"What?" Bon Tap wondered.

"You're *that* guy," Slicker hissed in the way Ixtalis spoke. "The one with all the questions."

"Am not!" he shot back, spine rigid and head thrown back. "Am I?"

He laughed with the group.

Danger. Combat. Those were the situations when true warriors found their humor. Their ability to focus sharpened to where they could switch from one topic to the next in an instant, never losing sight of what they were there to accomplish. The Bad Company at its finest.

"Make sure your shipsuits are intact and ready for deployment. Keep your beacons close at hand," Bundin ordered the group. "Continue scanning and searching. Dionysus, can you find out where the *War Axe* is going and why?"

"They are headed to the asteroid field, where they intend to fill the hangar bay with asteroids that they'll then use like shotgun pellets, if I have gotten correct the term Colonel Walton used."

"Fill the area with a fast-moving dust cloud that will reveal a spaceship that is hidden from all waveforms," K'Thrall postulated.

"I think we may be important to that effort since we can take a side view, as it may be." The Ixtali's statement gave the others pause, but after consideration, they agreed.

"Put us where we need to be to support that effort," Bundin ordered.

"We shall be a leaf on the wind," Dionysus replied.

"I'm sure that means something," Bundin started, "but I have no idea what it is. Are there any mechs on board?"

B'Ichi tapped the squad leader's shell as he climbed over. "I'll check," he said as he moved down the corridor to look for the main hold.

"I hope there are," Chris said softly. "I've never fought a spaceship before, but imagine if we could get on board like

Colonel Walton and the leadership of the Bad Company did to us when we were under Ten's control. I want to be more like him."

"I think he wants us all to be more like him. Fearless, leads from the front. He doesn't make us do anything he isn't willing to do himself. That's different than anything a Malatian would do. The higher up you go, the farther you get from the action."

"We've been given a gift," Bundin suggested. He craned his neck forward to stick his stalk head through the hatch to the bridge. Even though he spoke through a device attached to the bottom of his shell, his voice reverberated throughout the small space. "We were selected because each of us brings something different to a specialized operation. In a battle on a mountain, I'm useless, but underground or in space, I can serve. K'Thrall brings systems expertise, and also a Yollin carapace and mandibles. Slicker can climb and move in ways that none of us can, and she sees and senses things because of her innate spider-sense. Bon Tap, you're lean and faster than most. You bring the power of language and flair. One never knows how important that might be. Chris, our sole human, was a subject of an evil AI. He has an understanding we can't duplicate. And the Keome? He can live and work easily in places that would boil the rest of us alive. Together we're better than we are alone."

"We are in position, and powering down systems to reduce our energy signature. Maybe he won't notice us," Dionysus offered.

"Why is that ship following us?" the commander demanded to know.

"There is no confirmation that he can see us," the pilot replied, using passive voice to keep himself off the skyline.

"He is powering down his systems. And he's gone," the scanner operator reported.

"Find him!"

"Minimal active scans. Yes, Lord Mantis."

"Belay that," the commander replied.

"What weaponry did that ship have?"

"Scans were inconclusive," the operator answered, cringing in advance of the expected tirade.

"Why is that?"

"It is shielded somehow. Different from the others."

"They have a special ship that can see us but can also hide from us. It was waiting for us during our attack on the station, almost like it knew we would be there. We have a leak. We have a spy on board, or the ship's computer has been penetrated. I don't believe in coincidences. Review all emanations from the ship since we departed the attack point, Dulisto. Find me that leak."

"It will be done," the scanner operator replied before turning to his grim task of looking for a mole he didn't believe existed.

The commander contacted the weapons bay where the mines were stored. "How many remain?" he asked.

The weapons specialist was elbow-deep in attaching a magnetic grapple to a mine. When he couldn't extricate himself quickly enough to reply, he tasked one of his people to answer.

"Lord Mantis, this is a weapons technician answering on behalf of Weapons Specialist Katamara. There are six mines left to reconfigure, and that includes the two that were recovered previously."

"Why aren't you doing the work instead of the specialist?"

"The degree of experience necessary to keep from blowing up the ship is beyond me, Lord Mantis."

The commander clicked his teeth together and rolled his mouth as he contemplated the reply. "Learn. But don't blow up my ship." He signed off.

The weapons specialist breathed a sigh of relief because that was the greatest concession they would ever get from the commander. "Come and join me. It's time you learned how to do this."

The technician nodded and joined the specialist at a temporary workbench in the middle of the space. The open mine sat on it. Around them, the remainder of their active inventory was well-ordered on racks. Should there be an accident, they would all blow, and the ship would be vaporized.

"First step is to control your fear. Follow the steps in order, and you will be successful every time. Put your doubts aside and dig in. Take that curved slash and lean in here..."

"We need to reconfigure the hangar bay?" Kimber didn't understand the order. "Asteroids?"

TH explained his plan.

"We can always launch the drop ships—the Pods in their tubes—but the warriors in their armor will be at a disadvantage."

"No one is allowed on the hangar deck who isn't in armor. We'll need Aaron and Yanmei to launch in their fighters and remain outside the ship. They will be able to bounce our sensors and help us see if a shadow appears. Their firepower can be added to ours."

"Are they awake yet?" Kimber wondered. Last she'd heard, all those who had gone on a team jaunt into the Etheric were exhausted. Joseph and Petricia's suits stood empty near the inner bulkhead.

"I just roused them. They're on their way to the mess deck to load up on coffee."

"Any of the others?"

"Not yet." Terry tried to sound reassuring. "Do what you can to get the hangar deck ready. We'll be rendezvousing with Sue and Timmons any minute now, and they'll direct us to the smaller rocks. Expect an hour or so before we'll need the deck clear."

"Clearing the decks, aye aye, sir," Kimber replied, taking pleasure in using the phrase she'd seen in an old Earth movie.

"Well done," Terry Henry replied. "I'll try to get the others up too, but you know what good sleepers Joseph and Petricia are."

"They slept for fifty years once, didn't they?"

"They did." Terry shook his head, but he was smiling. "We may have to count them out for this one. In any case, the department heads will probably know the answers instead of us spinning our wheels."

Commander Suresha, who was in charge of the propulsion systems, was first into the hangar bay. She was followed closely by Commander MacEachthighearna, who was called "Mac" by everyone because no one could pronounce his full name. He was in charge of the environmental controls, or as Terry liked to put it, keeping the crew alive.

Commanders Blagun Lagunov and Oscar Wirth arrived together. One was Structure, and the other was Stores. They pointed and talked hurriedly to each other, nodding and providing counterpoints as they walked. When they reached Terry and Kimber, they stopped talking and waited.

"Thanks for coming," the colonel told them. "Whatever technology they're using, they are able to defeat all of our electromagnetic wave systems, from ultraviolet and x-ray through infrared and beyond, all the way to millimeter wave, and even more importantly, it stymies the Etheric, too. So, we're going to go old-school on them since we have an idea of where this ship is. We're going to blast as much rock as we can toward them and look for the shadows."

"They can block waves but not physical objects?" Suresha asked.

"Not just that," Terry replied, "they are invisible. We can see stars through them, but the ship is solid, as we found when Shonna and Merrit crashed a shuttle into it after it disappeared.

"Interesting. Sounds like a dark matter system. I wonder how they stabilized it? Is there any way you can capture it so I can study their technology?"

Terry's mouth fell open as he looked for the right response without sounding like an asshole. All he wanted was for the enemy ship to die. When they'd attacked the station, they'd relinquished their right to mercy.

"We'll do our best," he finally replied in an even voice. Suresha seemed satisfied with his answer. She stepped back, crossed her arms, and looked at the deck plate, all the while mumbling to herself about the possibilities of dark matter energy systems.

Terry turned to Blagun and Oscar, Structure and Supply. "Can we do it?"

"The asteroid thing?" Blagun Lagunov asked as his reply. "Sure. We can load up asteroids in here. I suggest keeping the gravity off so they float. We can energize the buffers to keep them from bouncing off the walls. What do you say we partition out some sections?" He pointed at regular intervals to mime five separate storage areas.

"Yes." Oscar nodded and followed the pointing fingers. "Take a fast run and eject the asteroids, then back up and hit them with some firepower. They'll already have some forward momentum, then you blast them into a billion pieces, which form a cloud of dust traveling through space at ten or twenty percent of light speed. Should smash into anything out there. What if the rocks destroy him?"

"Wouldn't that be something?" Blagun exclaimed, walking toward the hangar bay door. "You attack us, so we'll destroy you with a boulder!"

Terry saw the humor in it, and although he could hope, he expected to hit the enemy ship with overwhelming firepower the instant they could pinpoint where it was.

"Something like that," TH remarked. "Can you guys rig the forcefields to protect the walls and section off the stones we collect?"

"Sure. With Smedley's help, it'll take about fifteen minutes," Oscar replied. Terry gave him two thumbs-up, and they both hurried away.

Mac lingered. "What are you thinking?" Terry asked.

"Why?" the commander replied. "Why are they doing this? I saw your face when Suresha asked if you could take him alive. There's no way, but how many other ships are like that one? There's information we need, and there's only one place to get it."

"The enemy ship." Terry whistled his dilemma. "I know you're right, but I also know that this jagoff fired on our station. I can't let that go unpunished."

"What if they aren't deterred by that? What if it only emboldens them to return in greater numbers? How many invisible ships can we handle?"

Terry scowled at the series of questions. "I wish you weren't right. What happened to the good old days where you killed your enemy in a fair fight, then everyone went on their merry way?"

"Those days never existed."

"Dammit, Mac! Stop being right." TH clapped the man on the shoulder. "We'll do everything we can to disable that ship and seize it for the information we need to better prepare us to deal with this race of aliens."

"And probably any other alien race, too," Cory said

softly from the shadow of a parked mech suit. "Aliens need to know that we aren't a threat but we'll retaliate if attacked, even though we prefer to talk first. I think more races than not will respond to a play-nice strategy."

"But these guys..." Terry was at a loss. No one had been killed, even on the station. "Maybe they *are* sending us a message of peace. I wish we spoke their language."

"Joseph?"

"He was able to talk to Bundin before anyone else. Maybe, but that means we need to capture one of them. I would prefer all of them, after disabling their ship. We want their invisibility system. I'm sure Ted would love to tear it apart, and Suresha will be right there with him."

"Then why don't you do that?" Cory wondered, followed by a single-shoulder shrug.

"If it were that easy, it would already be done." Terry looked out the open hangar bay door. "Kimber. Suit everyone up, and prepare for zero-gee and no atmosphere."

Kimber saluted and strode off to find the nooks and crannies the warriors had found to sleep. She'd get Smedley to double-check since they couldn't stand to lose someone to carelessness.

Not on her watch.

"Let's get some rocks, shall we?" Terry said as he headed for the hatch on his way back to the bridge. "As Lord Byron said,

The night
Hath been to me a more familiar face
Than that of man; and in her starry shade
Of dim and solitary loveliness
I learned the language of another world."

As a Marine and a security professional, undercover operations had been his forte. Now was the time to use that expertise to battle an enemy who was better at hiding and better at staying in the shadows.

But not better than me, Terry snarled internally.

CHAPTER ELEVEN

"Mine L7-23U has been disabled and reconfigured with a magnetic grapple. 24T is next up for recovery," Katamara reported. He understood it was better not to try to keep secrets from the commander.

Lord Mantis accepted the information without comment.

"Grapples were installed on all the unrecovered stock." With the weapons technician's help, they were able to cut the time to less than half of what it took to convert a mine. They were finally caught up and able to convert the ordnance as soon as it was recovered.

"Your work is setting the *Traxinstall* up for a decisive battle with the enemy. We'll unleash these weapons in the right places at the right times, and the enemy will flee before us."

"For the glory of Myriador!" the technician shouted.

The commander walked out of the weapons bay. He liked to check on the workforce personally. He assumed it motivated them when he provided personal encouragement.

For the glory of Myriador, indeed. To memorialize Mantis forever. That was the only glory he sought, something he would never utter out loud. The crew and the ship would be soon be forgotten, but his name would live on.

Forever.

Lord Mantis strolled toward the bridge. One hundred and nine Myriador counted on him to lead them to victory and take them home. Their supplies floated out there somewhere, necessary provisions for the four-year return trip—unless they could secure a Gate drive like that little ship had. He was sure of it.

Their scans had been inconclusive, but the power signature of that tiny vessel rivaled that of the *Traxinstall*. They might be able to seize the ship intact. A plan started forming in his mind. Would he need to destroy the enemy if he could steal one of their Gate drives? Then the massed forces of Myriador could return in days, not years.

The thought was intoxicating.

For the glory of Myriador.

Terry and Timmons shook hands before Sue led the way onto their small survey vessel.

"Smedley, stay at a respectful distance until we call you in to collect the rock."

The AI affirmed the order. The ship took off from Spires Harbor and headed straight for the nearby asteroid field. After a few minutes, they turned to fly parallel to the last of open space along the rocky belt within this sector of the Dren Cluster.

"There's an area of smaller asteroids up ahead. We usually steer clear of it, since we need the quantities of ore available on the bigger ones. The small ones are dangerous, so of course, that's what you want." Timmons pointed an accusing finger at TH.

"This guy has been here long enough, and I've had all I can take of him." Terry chewed the inside of his cheek while he looked out the porthole at what had to have been a planet at some point in time. "It's the only thing I can think of. The only proposal that gives us something to do besides wait around to be attacked."

"I'd rather be doing something, too," Sue agreed.

Terry activated the comm system in the survey vessel. *"Ramses' Chariot*, this is Colonel Walton. Any change in the status of our intruder?"

The response was dead air and silence.

"Bundin?"

More silence.

Terry called the *War Axe*. "Do you have a fix on *Ramses' Chariot*?"

Micky's voice came through loud and clear. "We'll talk about how you abandoned the bridge without notifying me later," the skipper started. Terry painted a close-lipped smile on his face but didn't bother to argue. "We have a fix, although he stopped squawking the usual IFF—identification friend or foe—signal."

"He's trying to hide from the enemy..." Terry didn't finish his thought as Bundin's deep voice broke through the chatter.

"*Ramses' Chariot* is on station. We have no hint that the enemy ship has done anything other than try to recover the remaining deployed mines," Bundin explained before K'Thrall interrupted.

"We have a dearth of data," the Yollin stated.

"Do your best," Terry said. "And watch your asses. You're the only target he has right now. Make sure you keep your shields in place."

Dionysus popped into the conversation. "The shields are not up, but this is a special ship, and the gravitic system can snap into place in six to seven nanoseconds. We know the ship has to appear to fire. There is a one-second window."

"What about the mines?"

"Activating gravitic shields now," Dionysus replied. "I should have taken into account the fact that four out of the five ships attacked were destroyed by mines. The surviving ship and the station were attacked by the plasma cannon."

"Can your shields survive a thermonuclear blast?"

"Of course," Dionysus said proudly.

"Make sure we don't test that out. Good hunting." The colonel signed off.

Sue pointed out the transparent aluminum window of the survey craft. The usual crystal clear image provided by cameras and viewscreens was replaced by something fuzzy and more distant. Terry liked the enhanced version, but he had a soft spot for the nostalgia of what he could see with his naked eyeballs.

"That's it?" he asked.

"Bring in the *War Axe* and scoop your shotgun pellets into that big mouth that is the hangar bay door," Timmons replied with an indiscriminate hand-wave toward the window before turning back to Terry Henry. "Why is this happening?"

TH kept looking out at the window as he answered his friend. "I would like to know too because then we could address what's got him spun up. But in the end, it doesn't matter. It's him against us. I'd like to think the 'us' part makes us stronger, even though he has a tool at his command that gives him a significant advantage. Still, we're going to win this. Smedley? Start collecting rocks."

The *War Axe* moved into the space vacated by the survey ship.

Hang on, you bastard, Terry told the enemy within his mind. *We'll be there in just a few to ruin your day.*

"What is the big ship doing?" the commander asked.

"Maybe that's how they refuel," the weapons specialist replied.

"I can think of no other reason." Mantis looked from the tactical display to the main screen and back again. "Since he's refueling, prepare for Attack Plan Foiloes. A soft strike on the station and then we hit the shipyard hard, starting with the biggest first. Prepare to fire the plasma cannon, and move the ship out of the minefield. Once we've taken our five shots, deploy the magnetic mines."

"Lord Mantis, if I may," Katamara interrupted with bowed head. "We could drop a magnetic mine on the enemy ship that is trying to tail us. It is different, and now, with its shields up, we can get a weapons lock on it. Their shields won't matter under the fury of a sun's inferno."

The commander considered the request while he berated himself for not thinking of it. In the end, only *his* name would be remembered, no matter who else contributed to the victory.

"Make it so," the commander ordered.

Katamara nodded, his fangs clicking as he tried to hide his joy at contributing even more to the battle with the aliens.

With his center hand on top of the globe and his side hands inserted into the weapons station, he rolled up the exact weapon to launch within the tube and sent the coordinates to the navigation station to ensure the heading was correct to send the mine on a ballistic trajectory toward its target. Final corrections would be made by the mine itself through activation of the magnetic grapples.

He also started the process of producing the plasma and charging the cannon's capacitors. It could handle the first four shots without recharging, but the fifth would come only after additional power was added. The fifth shot was always taken at a closer range because it was weaker, but by that point, the enemy would have been crippled. The last round was the death punch. A battleship still floated in the shipyard, having sustained all five impacts from the plasma cannon. The station was much larger and would take a while.

But they had time.

The *Traxinstall* started to move, casually and gracefully. It assumed a course directly for the energy signature nearby. For its small size, the amount of energy it generated was astounding.

"Slower," Katamara requested. The ship slowed appreciably. The weapons specialist wanted the mine to arrive at the enemy ship when they were ready to engage the station —two attacks that would appear to be simultaneous to confound the enemy. "Mine is released and tracking."

"To the station, mid-speed," the commander ordered.

Like an arrow seeking the bullseye, the weapon with its magnetic terminal guidance flew through the void of space, shielded from prying eyes, unerring in its mindless mission of destruction.

"An anomaly straight ahead." Dionysus broke the silence and boredom infecting the bridge.

"Report," Bundin ordered.

"No mech suits on board," B'Ichi said from the corridor beyond. Bundin waved his tentacle arms at the Keome to plead for silence.

"It registered as an energy signature no brighter than a handheld light, disappearing almost as quickly as it appeared," Dionysus explained. "Launching a drone and taking evasive action."

Without waiting, the ship lurched and dove, accelerating toward a Gate that appeared at a ninety-degree angle to their previous course. It bolted through, and the Gate slammed shut behind them. An instant later, they appeared on the far side of the shipyard, close to where the *War Axe* was loading up on asteroids.

"What was your analysis?" K'Thrall wondered.

"The energy signature traced a short line that was headed directly toward us. The drone will mimic our profile. Let's see if that was what I think it was."

"Enlighten us, please," Bundin requested.

"Wait for it," Dionysus said, expanding the image showing the space where they'd been on the screen. It looked black, with faint stars in the background. The screen flared white before returning to its normal image of interstellar space.

"Share that signature and all details with every ship of the fleet." Bundin gestured with one tentacle arm toward the main screen.

"Already done, Corporal."

"That alone was worth taking Ted's ship and facing his wrath," K'Thrall suggested.

"You've never faced Ted's wrath before, I suppose." Bundin started to wave his arms again while his stalk head swayed. A low and slow rumbling filled the corridor.

"Is that two slices of humor in one day from our squad leader?" Slicker turned to face her fellow four-legged squad member. "Where has Corporal Bundin gone?"

"Thanks for trying," Bon tap added. "It makes a big difference, and thank you, Dionysus. I don't think this ship would have survived that blast."

"It was significantly greater than I anticipated, although there was a seventy-four point two percent chance that the shields would have held."

K'Thrall stopped what he was doing and stared in shock. "We had a one in four chance to die one minute ago, and Bundin is making jokes?"

"But we *didn't* die," Bundin replied casually in his slow, even, mechanically accentuated voice.

"I love that!" the Ixtali exclaimed.

"What did I miss?" B'Ichi asked. "And when's lunch? Did anyone make sure we had food?"

Chris held his hand over his heart. "We've survived to fight another day, but we learned something important. I'm good with that. If I get the term right, it's what us grunts do: sacrifice for the greater good, using our bodies as shields before an advancing tyranny."

"We almost died!" K'Thrall had been less excitable on the *War Axe*, but his near brush with death when none of his compatriots were Captain San Marino or Colonel Walton made him warier of his mortality.

"You've been watching too many movies," Bon Tap told Chris.

"Where are we headed?" Slikira asked. "If the enemy ship was coming at us, he was moving. It's not a stretch to think he's headed back toward the station."

"He's already there," Dionysus reported ominously.

CHAPTER TWELVE

"Fire." The commander sat back and watched as the ship transitioned beyond the shield, fired, and disappeared back under its cloak.

The Myriador warship yanked sideways, taking a thirty-degree offset to its previous position to stymie the counterfire.

The response time from the enemy battlewagons had dropped to less than a quarter of a second between the escape maneuver and when the first lasers lanced through the space where *Traxinstall* had been.

"Increase stand-off distance by three hundred percent," the commander ordered. The ship maneuvered away from the station and hovered, using only control thrusters until it had a gap between the ships that were using their hulls and shields to protect the station.

"Fire."

The second attack sent a bolt of plasma into the station. It raced in through a previous strike and exploded well within the station. A jet of gases escaped from the shape in a fountain of fire, air, and debris.

Traxinstall had already moved directly overhead by the time the return fire blasted through the area, covering most avenues of escape. The enemy was getting smarter and firing in wider circles more quickly than before.

"Delay the final attack. Increase stand-off distance another two thousand percent."

"They'll be able to intercept the plasma ball," the weapons specialist blurted. The commander glared at the insubordination. "Silence!"

"My sincere apologies, Lord Mantis." Katamara quivered with bowed head while he waited for his punishment to be doled out.

"Hit the station with this next shot," the commander offered without following it up. The stick hung over the weapons specialist's head. There would be no carrot.

"Shall we also throw a mine? Given the penetration of that last shot, we could destroy the whole station with a single mine if we can lob it into the hole."

The commander waited to answer. He was thinking about it. His strategy would be defeated before he could finish the task of destroying the enemy. The sure way to guarantee the annihilation of the *Traxinstall* was to kill the families of those manning the warships.

He assumed the families were on the station. He didn't have to answer the question regarding the station's biggest vulnerability since a battleship positioned itself in front of the heavily damaged section, a physical barrier with shields extended.

"Not yet," the commander replied. "But soon."

He said that to assure the bridge crew that he wasn't contemplating defeat, but that he was a genius, thinking multiple steps ahead of them. Which he was, but he didn't consider himself one of the mental giants. He understood the tactics, especially when he developed them on the fly.

"When the command to fire is given, you'll fire and immediately return to the minefield to recover more of our weapons. Our next strike will be on the shipyard." He waited through the acknowledgments and then issued the order. "Fire."

"Dionysus? What the hell just happened?" Felicity asked from where she'd fallen. No one had remained standing after the latest blast. She felt light-headed from the concussive wave that had passed through this section of the station, and light on her back—until she started to float.

"Power sub-station four has been destroyed, and with it, major sections of decks nine and ten. We've lost one gravity control module, too.

"Thank God!" Felicity exclaimed.

"I don't understand. We sustained major damage with that last attack. Battleship *Suvorov* has assumed station in front of the crater until repair bots can stitch together a new skeleton and skin."

"Thank God, because Ted's lab used to be in that section. If he wasn't on board the *War Axe*, he would be floating out in space somewhere, dying until his nanocytes revived him, then dying again, as many times as he had the energy before he could no longer be revived," Felicity drawled.

"I understand. Yes, Ted's empty office and lab were casualties of the latest strike. I have no data to surmise whether the enemy knew about the lab."

"I doubt it. I can't believe we have a traitor on board."

"It could be anyone passing through. This was a risk when the Gate was constructed and Keeg Station added to the star map."

"You're saying this is my fault?" Felicity struggled to her feet just so she could jam her fists to her hips and glare at the wall from which Dionysus' voice projected. She kept her movements slow and deliberate to prevent launching herself toward the ceiling.

"It was inevitable that characters you don't want to come calling would, once they had your address."

"That sounds very old-Earth of you," Felicity replied. "Do you think this has something to do with that? Who are these people?"

"Aliens. Their ship is like nothing we've ever seen before, and their cloak technology is beyond anything we've encountered. Maybe they have been around longer than we know, since we haven't been able to see them? What was the single event that caused them to go on the attack? That is what I want to know."

"Will we ever know that?" Felicity relaxed at the concession of the inevitability of this conflict, regardless that it was her efforts to build a Gate and make the station part of the expanding Federation that might have been the proximal cause. "Never mind. Connect me with Ted, please."

"He is on," Dionysus replied since Ted would pick up but not say anything.

"Ted, honey. We've taken some terrible damage to our lovely station. Tell me that this will all be over soon."

"I can't tell you that," Ted said, sounding like he had something in his mouth.

"Why not, dear?" Felicity had learned never to accept the short answer from her husband. He was often too literal, but she had gotten used to it and never took it personally.

"Because I haven't figured out how to find him. Plato and I are committing everything we have to this one magnificent problem. I need to get back to it. I hope to be home for dinner."

"He has signed off, Madame Station Manager," Dionysus remarked.

"God bless his soul. That's my husband." Felicity looked at the wall and turned to find the group of evacuees watching her. "He'll try to be home for dinner. Understand, good people of Keeg Station, the very best minds that the Bad Company has to offer are on this. Soon, we'll be able to go see what the damage is and start the healing and recovery process."

She beamed her best smile, but deep down it bothered her that Ted had not yet come up with a solution. He'd been working on it for half a day. He'd been quicker to crack Ten's security and make it possible for Terry Henry Walton to seize control of the Harborian fleet.

An entire fleet! This was one ship.

Had Ted met his match? She turned away from the others as worry creased her brow and knotted her stomach.

Aaron and Yanmei were half-asleep in the cockpits of the Black Eagles. They had stopped trying to fly a combat patrol around the *War Axe* and settled for remaining on station, moving every few minutes in a random direction to stymie the terror ship.

Char had returned to the bridge to be with Terry Henry, while Christina, Joseph, and Petricia had gone to the hangar bay and suited up, standing ready in their armor in case they were needed. The entire company was suited and ready for action.

Cory and Kai waited in the wings. Cory, in case someone got hurt. Kai, in case someone needed something. The drop cans were stored farthest from the hangar bay door, and completely blocked in until the asteroids were ejected. Dust filled the air from the rocks in the bay.

"If Dad wants a dust cloud, he's going about it in the right way."

Kai nodded in reply. "Smedley is going to have a cow when he's told to clean this up." Kai turned away from the mess that was the hangar bay. "Is this going to work, Auntie Cory?"

"That makes me sound old." Cory shook her head. She didn't know. She barely understood what the plan was because no one was sharing. They were running back and forth and throwing a lot of mud at the wall, hoping something would stick. She wasn't sure it would.

"You are old," Kai said, softly punching Cory in the shoulder.

"So are you, brat." Cory ruffled Dokken's ears.

I'm not that *old,* he interjected.

"Of course, you aren't." Cory leaned down to kiss the top of his head.

"All hands, the station has been attacked again. There's been a major breach of the interior, and they only have partial gravity. No lives lost. I say again, no lives lost," Colonel Walton reported over the ship-wide broadcast.

"Substantial damage," Kai repeated softly. "Is this guy toying with us?"

"I wish I knew. I wish I knew what was up with my dad, too."

Terry stood tall on the bridge, watching the moving parts of the entire tactical screen. He pieced together the images in his mind, creating a three-dimensional map within which he flew the *War Axe* to locations for optimal asteroid release. Three spots to send the three unique stores of stone and dust.

"Take us to these coordinates," Terry pointed to the holo-screen in front of the pilot and navigator positions. He put his finger on the spot he wanted. Clifton started tapping his screen, and the ship smoothly accelerated. "Prepare for deployment."

"Are you sure the ship will be there?" Micky asked.

"He just attacked the station. Last time he did that, it was a feint before he conducted a secondary attack. Move Alpha and Beta Squadrons to the station."

"Roger, Colonel," Smedley replied.

"Let's put up enough metal and interlocking gravitic

shields to keep the station safe. Delta Squadron is to take up a position around the hub of Spires Harbor."

"*Ramses' Chariot*, report," the colonel requested.

"Nothing new, Colonel," Bundin replied.

"Roger. Out." Terry studied the three-dimensional holographic tactical display. The two squadrons of Harborian ships moved agonizingly slowly at the scale shown. He knew they were accelerating at maximum. Delta Squadron was fumbling around, onesy-twosy-ing into place the twenty ships that should have moved in unison. "We need more training."

"The Harborians have had almost none." Micky defended the refugees, rescued recently enough that he was amazed they were able to function at all, let alone as a military unit. "Dionysus is mostly in control. The hands are back to doing what they did under Ten—repairs and maintenance according to exact instructions. Is taking their free will more important?"

"As long as we make sure we have a true crisis, then we are on solid ground. When the definition of a crisis changes to suit our desires to control others, then no. Right now? I'd order everyone to link arms and stand tall if that's what it took to save what we've built here. There are too many lives at stake to be sensitive to feelings. I don't want to lose the station or another ship."

"I understand, but I want to make sure that they do too." Micky folded his arms and waited—not in a power pose, but as a blanket of security. He couldn't advise TH about what to do because he didn't know.

The ghost in the dark was starting to give him nightmares. Not enough sleep and too much tension. Where would the beast strike next?

"Put me on open broadcast if you would, Smedley," Terry ordered.

"Ready," the AI replied.

"All hands on all ships, and our guest, who seems to be taking great pains to avoid loss of life: we are in this together. We are fighting for what we have and what we believe. We don't know why this ship is stalking and attacking us. He has kept us in the dark, but little by little, we're closing the noose. Soon, he'll have nowhere to run. It would be best if he talked to us before he becomes nothing but space dust."

Terry drew a finger across his throat.

"Broadcast is ended."

"I hope he understands Galactic Common or one of a million other languages. I can send him a translator if he needs it. All he has to do is make nice." TH studied the holo image, disappointed by how far away Alpha and Beta Squadrons were from the station.

I see clearly now, but what if the fog comes back? Terry kept his thoughts to himself. There was no need to concern Char or Cory. Not now.

The battle had not yet been joined.

It was time to fight back.

"There is debris where there shouldn't be debris," K'Thrall reported. "Dionysus, analyze these scans."

The Yollin tapped his screen, highlighting data obtained during the last active scan.

"We need a closer look. Wait one." The crew looked at each other. They never liked it when the AI told them to wait. A high-pitched warbling beep filled the bridge.

"What is that sound?" Bundin asked.

"That is a beacon attached to the canisters and crates." Dionysus didn't explain.

Bundin's stalk head started waving erratically. "Don't make me play twenty questions with you, Dionysus. What canisters and crates?"

"I presume they were jettisoned or inadvertently lost from the enemy ship, but they are in the area cordoned off by the *War Axe*. It is off-limits to all activity."

"Contact the *War Axe*."

"The communications links are not active."

"How does that work?" K'Thrall interrupted. "That should never happen."

"I cannot break through the static."

"Where is the static coming from?"

"Residual effects from the earlier blast, I believe," Dionysus explained.

"We didn't have this problem closer to the explosion." Bon Tap was confused. The others joined him.

"We've moved back into the area. For some reason, the radiation is concentrated in a small area, as if it's attached to something."

"How about we move away from that something and collect those supplies, then beat feet to parts unknown?" Chris offered.

"I assume you're speaking a common language, but

can't be sure," Bundin said slowly as he tried to parse the words and understand. "Moving from this area is our first priority. Make it so, Dionysus."

"Overriding command off-limits area on your authority, Corporal Bundin." Dionysus backed *Ramses' Chariot* away from the static and gave it a wide berth on their way to the beacon.

"You make it sound like you're recording the order to be used at my court-martial." Bundin's voice was deep, and it resonated throughout the corridor.

"Chow?" B'Ichi asked.

"I'm for that," Bon Tap agreed. Slicker stood as if the order had been given.

"We're heading toward the minefield to recover whatever is out there that the alien thought was important enough to attach a beacon to, and you want to eat?" Bundin asked in surprise.

"Dionysus, do you need us for anything related to this recovery?" K'Thrall clarified.

"I do not."

"See?" The Yollin joined the others. "If we're going where we're not supposed to go to do what needs to be done, then waiting on the bridge for something bad to happen isn't going to make it less bad when it happens. We might as well eat lunch, so we're ready in case there is something we need to do."

"I like your reasoning. Lunch it is," Bundin agreed.

The squad helped the Podder down the corridor to the small mess deck, which B'Ichi had confirmed was indeed stocked with source material for the food processor.

"Once we're clear, make sure the *War Axe* knows everything you know," Bundin yelled down the corridor, even though Dionysus could hear him wherever he was on the ship.

"It is mine to serve the whims of the warmbloods," the AI replied within the empty bridge. "Let's go fishing and see what we can catch."

CHAPTER THIRTEEN

"This message was different," the navigator said. "It came in on my channels, and it was one individual speaking briefly. We don't have anything that can translate their guttural gibberish."

"I'm sure it's nonsense." The commander waved his center hand dismissively. "Ignore it."

"Recovery of L7-24T is in process," Katamara announced to the bridge from his post in the weapons bay.

"The small ship is moving toward our beacon," the pilot reported.

"Stop recovery and target that ship."

"No!" Katamara shouted. "The mine is half in the tube. If we move now, it could blow. Just a little more time."

The commander seethed. They were following his orders, but he had to destroy that ship.

"Hurry up."

"Yes, Lord Mantis," the weapons technician replied after a short delay. The specialist was concentrating on his job of deactivating the weapon. It had to be done right.

"Will that ship contact one of the mines?"

"It will be close, but unless it changes course, it will not be impacted by any of the static mines."

"Prepare to fire the plasma cannon."

"Almost there," the technician reported.

"If that ship steals our supplies, we're as good as dead. Counting down. Firing in five...four...three...two...fire."

The weapons specialist's sigh filled the ship as he finished the sequence to disarm the mine less than a heartbeat before the mains cycled enough energy through the bay to make his skin tingle.

The ship remained visible as it fired a second shot at the small but resilient alien vessel.

The return fire caught the *Traxinstall* off-guard as the commander moved the ship deeper into the field.

Pulse weapons stitched across the prow, one impact penetrating deeply enough to open the hull to space. Atmosphere shot through the small opening like paint from a spray nozzle, but the automated sealing systems kicked in as the plasma cannon fired a third time.

The alien ship lunged toward the *Traxinstall*, vulnerable as it hung in space, a belligerent mouse trying to win a gun battle against an upstart alien with a huge power signature.

The commander guided the ship sideways. The alien ship fired again, impacting the mine positioned right in front of it. The explosion sent the ship spinning away.

"Shield," the commander ordered, and the *Traxinstall* disappeared. "Navigate to the jetsam beacon and recover our supplies."

"The enemy ship still lives!" the navigator exclaimed, not believing his own eyes.

"Launch a magnetic mine. Once the supplies are secured, take us back into the field—toward the other end this time. It's best not to remain on the battleground once victory has been declared. On to the next phase of this operation."

"Maybe it would have been better on the bridge," Bon Tap lamented as he cradled his broken arm. A gash down the side of his face dripped his blue Malatian blood.

Bundin was splayed across the two small tables in what passed for the mess deck on *Ramses' Chariot*. Lights flickered. The ship was spinning slowly through space, but at least the gravity system was intact.

K'Thrall, whose carapace had protected him, offered to help extricate the others from where they'd been thrown.

Slicker found herself on the wall, her ability to defy gravity on full display, but one of her legs dangled helplessly while the other three did the work of supporting her. Chris was out cold. K'Thrall lifted him from the deck and laid him beside Bundin.

B'Ichi stood. "Ain't this some shit?" he said, using the human vernacular as he pointed to a rip in his heating suit. He started to shiver, to the point that he was unable to do anything else.

The Podder flailed his legs until K'Thrall rammed a shoulder into him to drive him off the table, sliding him to the deck. Once upright, Bundin leaned close to the Keome and used two of his four tentacle arms to pinch B'Ichi's suit shut.

"Duct tape," Bundin requested.

Slicker slowly climbed down, found a roll of duct tape —standard issue for all warriors, and common in every space on a Bad Company vessel—and started to tear off strips. In short order, they had the Keome's suit repaired.

"Let's take a look at that cut," K'Thrall told Bon Tap, demonstrating a soft side that no one had seen before. Doubling a napkin, the Yollin pressed hard on the wound. "Head injuries usually bleed at a rate disproportionate to the actual damage, so it looks worse than it is."

He applied duct tape to hold the napkin in place before looking at the Malatian's arm.

"Stop the bleeding, start the breathing, protect the wound, and treat for shock," Slicker recited the training that had been driven into them as part of being a warrior under Colonel Walton's command. "I'm thinking we don't have time for the shock part."

"Don't go into shock," Bundin deadpanned.

Slicker's arachnid eyes whirled at the humor of his statement. "I'm not sure that's how it works."

"Dionysus, status," Bundin requested, hoping the AI was still with them.

"Automated systems are engaged. Engines are offline as a precautionary measure while diagnostics are run on the converters, inverters, and power relays. Shields are in place, and the ship is in one piece."

"Is this what the seventy-fourth percentile looks like? It's that place between where we didn't get destroyed and we survived, but the how well we survived part wasn't clearly articulated." Bundin left it at that.

Dionysus tried to take the edge off the crew's angst.

"The weapon was extremely powerful. A lesser ship would not have survived."

"You're going to feel a little strain," K'Thrall said. Slicker grabbed the Malatian from behind and the Yollin yanked his broken arm, stretching the tendons until the bones aligned and settled into place. Bon Tap screamed until the shrill pitch assaulted their senses.

K'Thrall slapped him on the head. "Stop that."

Bon Tap gasped and panted.

"You could have let me know."

"So you could tense up? Nah. We don't have time to babysit, and if you scream like a Yollin schoolgirl again, I will jettison you out the airlock."

"No jettisoning," Bundin clarified. He worked his way to the table, where Chris was starting to stir.

"I must be in space," he mumbled.

"What?" the others said as one.

"I'm seeing stars."

"He's fine." K'Thrall pointed to Slicker's leg. "Let's take a look at that."

"Who would have guessed that K'Thrall would be the squad's medic?" Slicker turned to put her damaged limb on display.

K'Thrall knelt to take a look. B'Ichi grabbed her and held her tightly.

"Let me go, buffoon!"

"Aren't we going to do that thing you did to Boner?"

"No." K'Thrall shook his head. "This is something completely different. It seems to be dislocated, but I'm not sure if the tendons are torn, or if Ixtalis even have tendons."

"We do, but they're not like a humanoid's."

K'Thrall gently pushed the leg joint back into place despite Slicker's wincing and grunting. "Duct tape."

With B'Ichi's help, they taped the joint into place while keeping her leg supported.

"You won't be running any marathons, but that should keep it stable until we can get you into a Pod-doc."

Chris Bo Runner held his head while keeping his eyes closed. "Did we fire at it?"

"Good question. Dionysus?" Bundin relayed.

"Yes. We fired the pulse cannon that is under development. The enemy ship was hit multiple times, and at one point, it vented atmosphere. Unfortunately, we detonated a mine danger-close before the enemy ship cloaked. I detected another anomaly right before we detonated the mine, and have maneuvered us out of the estimated path."

"We hit it and hurt it. Are we able to contact the *War Axe?*"

"They are on their way. Colonel Walton has directed us to recover those supplies at all costs."

"Did he ask how we were?" Bon Tap asked, still suffering from spasms caused by the throbbing pain in his arm that radiated through his whole body.

"He knows that you are all alive," Dionysus replied. "He also knows that there is a new mine out here, floating around, invisible to our sensors. I've developed my estimate of its course and transmitted that to the fleet so that they remain clear."

"Good that a second mine didn't hit us and we're still alive. Everything else is gravy," Chris muttered from the table. He made no effort to open his eyes or move, just draped an arm over his face.

"I'll go to the cargo bay to ensure the recovery goes well. B'Ichi, you're with me. K'Thrall and Slicker, to the bridge. We have a mission, and we are not going to let the colonel down. Boner, you stay here and take care of each other. Chris? Don't die on us. Join them on the bridge when you're up to it. Otherwise, keep doing what you're doing."

"Aye, aye, Corporal," Chris said with a weak salute. Bon Tap nodded before pouring water for himself and the Harborian.

"Let's see what he was willing to die for," Bundin said as the squad members executed their orders.

"The big ship is returning," the navigator reported, "and it appears to be assuming station on the far end of the field."

"Like jockeys on ramsteeds preparing to joust?" the commander speculated. "Now that he has restored his energy, he thinks that he is in a position to best us?"

No one replied. The commander was learning that when he shut down any input from his crew, they stopped providing it. He had started to miss the weapons specialist. The upstart was the only one who was honest, and his comments helped the commander to understand.

"Specialist Katamara to the bridge. I want your opinion on what the enemy ship is doing." There. He had told the entire crew that he couldn't do all the thinking for them. That he was fallible. He had recruited the best and the smartest for this mission, then treated them like drones. With the last engagement and the damage they'd taken, his mortality was front and center in his mind.

Not only would he die, but he'd also take the ship and the crew with him. On Myriador, they would simply be the ship that never returned. There would be no glory, just a forgotten plaque on a nondescript wall gathering dust. Crying families. A government payout.

The recovery of the supplies was quick. The crew breathed a collective sigh of relief, until they found that twenty percent of the crates had been destroyed by the big ship's massive railgun. That meant reduced rations for almost a full year, but they could go home.

All of them.

"Heading into the field," the navigator said with more energy than before. Hanging the supplies over their heads like a guillotine to get them to perform their duties had not delivered the zeal and commitment the commander had hoped for. In fact, it had had the opposite effect. The crew was cowed and docile.

The crew had been afraid. The commander had felt fear, too.

The bridge's hatch opened, and the weapons specialist walked through.

"Katamara," the commander started. The bridge crew tensed. Most didn't think the commander knew their names, let alone said them aloud. "The big ship went into the asteroid belt and has now returned. It took no action when we attacked the station."

The weapons specialist was on edge. "Please allow me to contemplate the information, Lord Mantis."

The commander waited while they both studied the tactical display.

"The enemy ship is accelerating beyond what is possible!" the navigator exclaimed.

"If he is doing it, it is not impossible," the commander corrected. "It's not possible for us, you mean."

"The ship has come to an abrupt stop and is ejecting what appears to be bits and chunks of asteroids. They've fired their capital-grade weapons at the asteroids." The navigator leaned close to his scope. "They've sent a massive debris cloud toward the minefield at two percent of light speed."

"I guess that answers what they're doing," Katamara said. "Physical objects like gravel and dust will show them where all of our shielded mines are."

As if to confirm his statement, the debris cloud passed a mine, creating an eddy out of the dust. A single shot from the primary weapon destroyed the mine. The big ship followed the cloud at a discrete distance, blasting the exposed weapons as they went.

"Move us out of the debris cloud's course." The commander crossed his arms, resting his third arm in the hammock created by the other two. He clacked his fangs in frustration. "Take us behind that ship, as close as you can get us."

The large ship dashed forward and released more stone, firing again to accelerate the smaller particles. The navigator adjusted their trajectory to keep the *Traxinstall* out of the path of the debris.

A third cloud was formed, and the ship seemed to revel in destroying the mines. It happened so fast that the *Trax-*

install hadn't gotten where it needed to go when the alien ship accelerated toward the shipyard at a pace where the Myriador vessel couldn't keep up.

"Break off pursuit," the commander ordered. "Take us to their Gate."

The ship maneuvered away. The commander needed time to think.

"Let us plan our next series of attacks," he told the weapons specialist. "The goal for this next phase is to destroy as many of the enemy ships as possible while limiting our own exposure. We have repairs we need to finish before we go face to face with the enemy."

"I could not agree more, Lord Mantis." The weapons specialist was unsure of the commander's new direction. He expected it was to scapegoat him for the mission's failure, but on Myriador, the captain was always blamed.

Always.

"If we destroy the big ship, the others will fear, and then we'll have them, too."

CHAPTER FOURTEEN

Captain San Marino stood next to Terry Henry Walton as they studied the tactical grid like two master chess players. Each appearance of the alien ship was highlighted with a virtual pin and color. Where the minefield had been was displayed in yellow, with pinpoints of light where each mine had been.

The attacks were a flaming red that married up with the damage that had been done to the station or to a ship. In the void of space between the shipyard and the station, a lone red flag stood out, with multiple pins surrounding.

The short but intense battle that *Ramses' Chariot* had fought with the alien destroyer.

Terry expected the next report via Smedley from Dionysus.

"The alien supplies are gone, Colonel."

"Understood." Terry clicked his tongue as he disappeared into his own mind, trying to fill in the knowledge gaps with speculation that wasn't outrageous.

"But some material has been recovered that is foreign

to our space. I believe that it is from something destroyed when the *War Axe*'s mains hit the enemy ship."

"*Ramses' Chariot* hit that bastard, too." Terry never took his eyes from the display. "We have a ring of steel around the station. The minefield..."

He pointed to a large gap.

"The mines were laid in a regular pattern," TH said, still pointing, "so why is this gap here?"

"He recovered them," Micky said matter-of-factly.

"He laid the mines and then started recovering them. He threw a cloaked mine at the *Chariot*, which is what I suspect he did to these two ships here." The red flags highlighted the destroyed two ships that had been in cold storage and the heavily damaged but minimally crewed Harborian battleship.

"Passive mines and active mines." TH scratched his arm and wondered about when the last time he had taken a drink of water was. "There's only one enemy ship. He's not trying very hard to kill us, except the *Chariot*, and that was all about those supplies. We hit him in the storage hold, and he lost his stuff. He didn't need it right away, so he dropped a beacon on it. When the *Chariot* found it, he had a huge 'Oh shit!' moment, and then it became two junkyard dogs scrapping over the last chicken leg."

"If only he'd talk to us."

"I don't think he can," Terry replied.

The hatch to the bridge opened, admitting Char and Cory. Terry smiled. He knew what he was fighting for. He didn't need it to be in the middle of the battle or after a tragic loss. He was fighting for his family, and for those with families.

"If he can't talk, how do we get through to him?" Micky asked.

"That is the million-credit question." Terry waved at the ceiling as he did when trying to get Smedley's attention. "Ask Ted, Smedley. I don't want to interrupt him again."

Char and Cory both snickered at Terry's mannerism. A man of the future, stuck in the past. Whenever a comm link was established with Colonel Terry Henry Walton, Smedley added static and clicks although there were none just to make the old Marine feel more comfortable.

The two women joined Terry and Micky at the front of the bridge. Cory surreptitiously put her hand on her father's neck. Immediately, the soft blue glow began. Cory shot knowing eyes at her mother. Char's look of concern outweighed how tired she was.

"What's with all the touchy lately?" Terry ducked out from under Cory's hand and dodged out of the way. He assumed a position on the other side of Char, keeping her between him and Cory.

"We care about you. That shouldn't happen when Cory touches you. We need to get you into the Pod-doc to figure out what's going on."

"Later." Terry put his foot down.

"Stubborn jarhead."

"The one you've fallen head over heels in love with because I'm me." Terry smiled, dodging as Cory reached for him again.

"I'm sure that's it. It couldn't have been that you relentlessly pursued me from the moment you laid eyes on me until I finally settled."

"You're a fucking werewolf! I thought you were going to kill me in my sleep," Terry countered.

"Maybe I still am." Char raised one eyebrow and tipped her head down to look at her husband.

"You have the patience of Methuselah." TH made cow eyes at the purple-eyed werewolf.

"Enemy ship? Still out there? Still can't talk to him?" Micky droned.

"Right," TH replied, returning his attention to the tactical plot. "Where are you now?" he asked the enemy.

"We know where he wasn't. He either evaded the dust cloud or wasn't there in the first place. I have to say, although I was skeptical about filling my hangar bay with rocks, the end result was well worth the effort. We were able to eliminate the minefield, and if the premise that he was recovering them is correct, then we cut his supply of weapons to use against us." Micky snapped a quick salute. "I salute you."

"Thanks, Micky. That was the only arrow in my quiver. I got nothing else," Terry said using the colloquial speech he reverted to for self-deprecation.

"You don't have to know everything," Char suggested. "Smedley, what did Ted have to say?"

"He would *not* answer," Smedley said, enunciating each word.

"Time to put on my alpha hat," Char said. "Coming?"

Terry didn't feel like he had a choice. "Hold the fort, Micky. I'll be right back."

"Hold the fort. Let me say that again: hold the fort. Like when *I* told *you* to hold the fort, and returned to find you missing from the bridge? Have no fear, Terry Henry Walton, I will be on the bridge when you get back."

"What? Nothing got blown up. We were fine!" Terry left the skipper behind as he and Char headed for Combat Information, where Ted was deep in thought. Cory trailed behind them. TH quickened his pace to keep her from getting too close.

***

"I want to take out that big bastard," the commander said.

"Chasing his tail, we lead him into a magnetic mine. How many of those can he survive?"

"I don't want to fathom a guess. We need to hit him when he's not looking and shove a mine in through his front door. The hangar bay on that ship is perpetually open."

The weapons specialist manipulated a three-dimensional image of the heavy destroyer. "It has powerful forcefields to protect it *and* keep the atmosphere in."

"Do we know where the power source for the forcefields is?" the commander asked.

"Energy is off our charts in three different areas. That ship generates more power than all of Myriador combined."

"Then it'll make a magnificent explosion when it goes, will it not?"

"I would like to see that supernova, more so if it happens within the shipyard. The secondary explosions from the wave traveling through would be something to behold." The specialist was starting to believe it was possible to defeat the enemy.

"They'll replay it a hundred times a day back home."

"For the glory of Myriador," the weapons specialist cheered.

The commander had started to believe as well. Maybe it *was* possible to win. "Take us to the shipyard to send a mine their way, and then to the station to draw them to us, where we'll have more surprises in store."

"Yes, Lord Mantis!" the bridge crew cried in unison.

"For the glory of Myriador!" He thrust his center fist in the air, all the while watching the image of the alien ship grow larger on the screen as the *Traxinstall* flew toward it.

***

"What now?" Bon Tap asked from his seat in the captain's chair. K'Thrall and Slicker were in their positions at the front of the bridge. Pilot and Systems, although Slicker wasn't flying the ship. Dionysus was.

K'Thrall continued to study the data that flowed across the screen before him.

"Make like we're a hole in space and watch," Bundin suggested.

"All systems set to passive," K'Thrall replied. "Dionysus, any new information regarding the alien ship? We've seen it materialize a number of times now while under direct visual and technical observation. You have to have something."

"Materialize isn't the correct term. It's as if he's hiding behind a closed door that looks like the wall. When the door opens, we see. The rest of the time, it's closed and he is invisible to us. All the while, he has remained in place."

"A lot of words poured from the speaker, but I didn't hear any revelations," Bundin suggested, being more snarky than usual in his position wedged into the corridor outside the bridge.

"My apologies, Corporal Bundin. I don't have any revelations. We see for two fractions of a second when the enemy launches a mine toward us. Somewhere between the launch and it clearing the ship's cloak, it's visible, but only to sensors. Maybe that's a glitch when a cloaked entity passes through the other cloak. For that brief moment in time, they cancel each other out. We get two points of reference to give us a general trajectory."

"Outside of that, we have nothing," K'Thrall lamented.

"That's more than we had when we first flew out here. And we know that the enemy ship has been hit at least twice. Both times it vented, once supplies and the second time atmosphere." Bundin's tentacle arms ended with hands that he rarely rubbed together, but he did now, mirroring the human crossed-arms pose. His blue stalk head remained steady for an abnormally long time.

B'Ichi remained in the corridor and lounged ingloriously against Bundin's shell. There were at least two full rolls of duct tape holding his suit together. He looked like an alien from Earth's past.

He was in character.

"We could use a mech," Chris said from behind Bundin.

"We could, but we don't have one," the squad leader replied.

"Maybe we can rendezvous with the *War Axe* and suit up?"

"Dionysus, connect me to Colonel Walton."

It took longer than usual, and when the colonel finally answered, he sounded like he was in a corridor. "Report, Corporal."

"Request permission to dock with the *War Axe* to get a couple mech suits and then take *Ramses' Chariot* back to space."

"Granted, but make it quick. Meet us at Spires Harbor."

"Roger. Bundin, out." The Podder unfolded his arms, and his head started to wave about.

"Who's your daddy?" K'Thrall yelled.

"What the hell does that mean?" Slicker demanded. She reached across the ship's control panels to punch the Yollin in the middle of his chest carapace. Her hands were hard as iron, so it didn't hurt her. She hoped he felt it. He lifted his chin and clicked his mandibles at her.

"Set course," Bundin ordered.

"On the way," the AI responded.

"Boner, Chris, and Slicker, you're all going into the Pod-doc when we get back."

"We don't have time for that!" Chris countered.

"Who in the hell is going to suit up besides B'Ichi?"

The modified four-legged armored suits were not yet ready. The space suits were sound, but those weren't desirable for combat where there was even a remote chance of punching a hole in the suit. Duct tape didn't always solve problems.

"My head is clearing. Put Boner in first, then Slicker. If we run out of time, I'll make do."

"Are you sure?" Bundin studied the man's eyes.

"I don't want to miss this fight. Who knows what kind of shot we're going to get? We need to be ready. As the colonel says, we need to be firstest with the mostest."

"That's not grammatically correct," Dionysus remarked.

"Then you correct him." Chris closed his eyes and took deep breaths. The light and sound bothered him. Bundin didn't want him in the fight, but the Pod-doc could cure all ills—after the fact, if need be.

"I politely decline." The AI knew which battles were worth fighting.

"Prepare to disembark. We have no time to waste. Boner, Slicker, and Chris to sickbay. B'Ichi, get yourself into a hot mech, and K'Thrall, go to the CIC and see if you can help Ted."

"Isn't that a novel idea? But I accept the challenge, and volunteer as tribute," the Yollin replied.

"Just when I thought I was starting to understand you, I find that I don't understand anything," Bundin bemoaned. He watched in all directions with his four eyes as the squad vaulted and slid over his shell to get into position to race off the ship. Slicker moved slower than usual, but she was still faster than the Podder. K'Thrall supported her, and Bon Tap and Chris helped each other.

"Preparing to dock," Dionysus reported.

"With utmost haste, warriors," Bundin encouraged.

CHAPTER FIFTEEN

"The ship we fought earlier is on its way here," the weapons specialist announced. "What if it is headed into the hangar bay of the big ship?"

"Then it would be best for it to enter with a mine attached to its hull. A single mine will destroy both vessels. Make it so, Katamara." The commander spoke slowly and evenly.

"Deploying three mines with magnetic grapples and fuses set to delayed activation. Give him time to get inside the belly of the beast." The weapons specialist manipulated the controls at his station and sent three mines into the void to wait in front of the big ship's open hangar bay. "It was genius to come here. This will be a fatal blow to the enemies of Myriador."

"That is the plan," the commander said, watching the mines move into position before activating positional thrusters to remain in place. Three weapons, waiting for the unwitting to hitch a ride.

The small ship pulled up abruptly, stopping outside the

big ship's shields. "They are coordinating to drop their forcefield," the weapons specialist said hopefully.

"I don't think so. Get us out of here. Back to the station. It's time to wreak havoc." The commander waved his center arm at the pilot, who engaged immediately, almost jerking the crew off their feet. "That little bastard has seen the mines. I don't know how, but he has."

"Looking for vulnerabilities," Katamara stated as he manipulated the latest three-dimensional tactical image showing the station and the forty-five ships surrounding it. "Would they risk hitting their own ships?"

"As in, we get between them so they shoot each other while we hammer the station?" The commander looked at the image, but he saw only red. If he lost the ability to hide behind the shield, he would be vulnerable. If he was vulnerable, he was dead. The *Traxinstall* had already discovered that the alien weapons would shred its hull. He was one direct hit away from being nothing but a memory. "We won't take that risk. Not yet."

"Yes, Lord Mantis." The weapons specialist focused his anger as he racked up the target points on the station.

"And spread the pain on our way out of this shipyard."

Katamara chose a cold target, one he knew wouldn't fire back as they accelerated toward the station.

"Fire," the commander ordered.

<hr>

"I know they are there," Dionysus said. The squad was clustered in the corridor, waiting to leave the ship, and the abrupt stop had confused them. The AI clarified. "I'm coordinating with the *War Axe* now."

"Should we return to the bridge?" Bon Tap asked from where the others pressed him against the airlock. "Or maybe it's better to die in the corridor?"

"No one is going to die," Bundin replied.

"Standby with pulse weapons," Dionysus declared. "The *War Axe* is venting the last of the asteroid dust from the hangar bay."

K'Thrall extricated himself from the mass of bodies and hurried back to the bridge in time to see three shadows appear on the main screen. The destroyer's close-in weapon system lit up the mines, tearing them apart. Only one exploded.

"Secure and recover the unexploded ordnance," Dionysus said, giving a step by step for those not on the bridge.

A maintenance bot flew from a storage bay on the *War Axe's* hull. As it approached the last location of one of the destroyed mines, it sprayed paint in a wide cloud. The gray coated the larger pieces, now visible since the cloak had been deactivated or destroyed yet the parts had remained elusive.

"I've got you now," Dionysus remarked.

"By 'you,' you mean an unexploded thermonuclear warhead?" K'Thrall clarified.

"That would be 'you,' correct."

"Can we get off first?" Bon Tap asked.

The alien ship appeared for a moment, its plasma cannon burped, and then the ship disappeared. The *War Axe* responded, its auto-firing systems blanketing the area, but it was too late. The ship had been accelerating away from them.

"Any debris?" Micky asked.

"The enemy escaped unscathed," Ruzfell reported. "The Harborian frigate has been destroyed."

An image appeared on the screen showing a ship that had split in half, breaking into smaller pieces as the sections drifted, leaving a trail of debris in its wake.

"Let the station know the enemy ship is on its way," Micky said softly.

Terry opened the door to the CIC, and he and Char stepped in. The space was kept in perpetual twilight to ensure that every detail stood out on the myriad screens. Only Ted and the Crenellian were in there.

"Ankh! I didn't know you were aboard." Terry looked at the small alien and waited for a reply before realizing that none would be forthcoming. He didn't answer questions that weren't questions, and simply stated facts. What Terry did or did not know was irrelevant to the Crenellian.

"Go away," Ted said, cutting to the heart of Terry's visit.

"No." Two can play at that game. "The alien attempted to blow up your ship by dropping mines in front of our hangar bay. He probably hoped it would blow us up too when we created an opening in our gravitic shield for *Ramses' Chariot* to fly through."

"My ship shouldn't be out here," Ted argued.

"The *Chariot* has discovered things about the alien ship that no one else was able to find. Dionysus is in command of it, and is making sure it fights well. You trust Plato's stepchildren, don't you?"

"Of course, he does," a voice interjected through the overhead sound system. Plato, the AI that Ted created.

Ted's mouth worked as if he were going to say something, but no sound came out.

"I concur," a new voice joined. "Dionysus' performance during this crisis that is completely Colonel Walton's fault has been exceptional."

It was Erasmus, the AI that traveled with Ankh.

Char put her hand on Terry's arm, and he took a deep breath before asking, "How is this my fault?"

"It's always your fault whenever we're led into combat. Ergo, when in combat, it's your fault," Plato replied.

"That makes no sense. I was thinking about going on vacation. What if Char and I had been gone? This alien still would have attacked. No matter whose fault, *not mine*, we need a way to see this ship when he's cloaked."

"I'm working on it. Not right now, of course, because you're interrupting." Ted crossed his arms to make a show of not working.

Terry's hand twitched because it wanted to hit something. He unflexed his fist and smiled. Char wrapped her arm around his waist, pinching his butt on the way.

"Can we have every ship in the fleet fire at a variety of angles? We have all this firepower that's not being used. Better to look for a needle in a haystack, despite the remote chances of finding it, than to wait until you step on it."

"Kill that ship, Ted," Char said in a low voice.

"Space is a very large area," Ted started slowly. His eyes unfocused as his mind started to work. He was communing with Plato. Ankh stared at a spot on the wall as his mind and Erasmus' joined to figure out how to do it.

Ted pulled up holo screens, within which Ankh joined him. The two poked and tapped at the images in the air.

"And that's how the alpha does it," Char claimed.

"By looking mean at them?" Terry prodded.

"Letting my number two do the jousting until he's vulnerable, then swoop in for the kill."

"Will it work?" Terry asked, not talking about the alpha dog.

"With Ted and Ankh on it, chances are as good as they can be. What about the stuff the *Chariot* recovered?"

"Let's take a look." Terry and Char kissed, passionately as they always did, blocking out all around them as effectively as Ted and Ankh. Hand in hand, they quietly left the CIC, shutting the door gently behind them before hurrying down the stairs to the hangar bay.

"Are we sure that thing has been neutralized?" Bundin asked.

"I am one hundred percent certain," Dionysus replied. "Well, a solid ninety, at least."

"What?" Bon Tap started to panic.

"I jest. Did I get the humor right?"

"You almost gave me a heart attack, you digital dickweed!"

"Yes. I got it right. That is hard for me. I'm happy to be making progress. Access has been granted."

Ramses' Chariot moved toward the gaping maw of *War Axe*'s hangar bay doors. It had actual doors that could be closed, but with Ted's improvement of the gravitic shields, they rarely closed them anymore. The forcefield kept the atmosphere in while allowing ships to pass through, and the shields protected the whole ship from impacts of any sort.

K'Thrall joined the others waiting at the airlock.

"We're a hell of a lot closer than we were before to being able to find this guy," he offered.

"Why us?" Chris asked.

Bundin waved his tentacle arms to get everyone's attention. "It is as we've been taught and encouraged. Initiative, weighing risks versus reward, understanding the mission objective. By taking the *Chariot*, it put us in a position to collect data, and even land a couple blows for the good guys. Yes. We have done right by the Bad Company because we *are* the Bad Company."

"Corporal Bundin, I have to admit that I used to follow you out of curiosity, but now I'll follow you because you're a good leader."

"I don't know what to say to that," Bundin replied.

"Get the hell out of the way! All ashore who's going ashore," K'Thrall declared as the hatches popped and armor-suited warriors stomped across the deck toward them.

Bon Tap and Slicker stumbled out first, hurrying as best

they could with their injuries. Chris followed while B'Ichi and K'Thrall lifted and twisted to get the Podder through the narrow hatch. Once out, the Keome ran to get a suit of armor and K'Thrall made a beeline for the CIC. Bundin worked his way to the stern of the *Chariot*, where the warriors were helping two bots unload their hard-earned cargo.

The twisted pieces and wreckage didn't look intimidating, but Bundin knew better. The mine's small warhead had been stripped of its detonator and initiating hardware. It was nothing but an explosive now, harmless because there was no way it could detonate.

"What are those?"

A bot wrestled with two heavy metal strips that seemed to have a life of their own.

Private Gefelton, a warrior in a mech suit whose girlfriend was one of the ship's engineers, provided his insight. "Looks like a magnetic clamping device."

"Bundin to Colonel Walton," Bundin requested, using the hangar bay's comm.

"What do you need, Corporal?" Terry said as he and Char approached.

The Podder seemed unfazed that the colonel was there already. "Magnetic attachments." He pointed at the bot with the devices that kept trying to attach to it. "We pulled them from the mine wreckage."

"Is that why the alien recovered the mines? To put these things on them and make them into active weapons versus passive? Or was this just to sneak one aboard the *Axe*?"

"I think the latter," Char offered. She had earned an engineering degree a long time ago but was having trouble keeping up with the tech of the Etheric Federation.

Terry waved Char around one side of *Ramses' Chariot* and he ran around the other, examining it for any unwanted visitors. Once he finished with what he could see, he leapt to grab a handhold and pulled himself to the top of the ship to make sure nothing was up there, either.

He gave Char a thumbs-up. "Clean," he declared.

She nodded in agreement. The ship was clean. The three devices they had destroyed were the only ones, at least in close proximity to the *War Axe* and *Ramses' Chariot*.

"We need Ted and Ankh to take a look at this stuff," Terry said, wincing at the thought.

Char vigorously shook her head. "Once they have the firing plan completed, we'll turn them loose on it. In the interim, maybe Smedley can work with Plato and his stepchildren to study this stuff." She pointed at the collection of shattered metal, parts and pieces, and even a few bits of organic material.

"Take it all to the maintenance bay, where it can be scanned," Terry ordered.

The warriors in armor complied, moving the collection to two pallets and then carefully carrying them to the oversized hatch in the forward section of the hangar bay, right before the three drop ship tubes.

Terry jumped from the top of the ship, executed a somersault, and landed on his feet.

"Where did that come from?" Char wondered.

"Feeling good," he told her.

"Maybe if you'd smashed your face, you'd get in the Pod-doc so we can figure out what's wrong with you."

"Maybe there's nothing wrong with me," Terry countered.

"Then the Pod-doc won't find anything. Cory's worried. You trust our daughter, don't you?"

"That's a loaded question. I thought you trusted *me*." Terry held both her hands and looked into her purple eyes, lost afresh in the wonder of the swirls and the twinkle that appeared.

"I do," she said, her voice barely above a whisper. "I trust you with my life, but I don't trust you when it comes to yours. You are a terrible judge of whether you're fine or not. Marines and their tough-guy attitude. You people need the Navy to look after you."

"Whoa! Them's fightin' words." He found himself incapable of conjuring an angry face for Charumati.

"Pod-doc," she reiterated.

"When this is over," he replied, turning serious. "I am fine. At this moment, my head is clear, and my body is as sharp as it ever was."

"These people are depending on you. *I'm* depending on you." A tear glazed one eye. "You told Ted you were thinking of taking a vacation. I'm putting my foot down. We're taking one as soon as this is over, right after you come out of the Pod-doc. We'll take *Ramses' Chariot* and go to a pleasure moon somewhere."

"They have those out here?" Terry winked. "Maybe we can whip by Onyx Station."

"No. Absolutely not. We are not making our vacation a work trip. You'll start drinking with Nathan Lowell, and then who knows what will happen."

"Deal," he agreed—not that he had any choice in the matter.

"Maintenance bay?" Char asked. Terry had been inching toward the hatch while they talked.

"Never thought you'd ask. I'm in!" They walked hand in hand across the hangar bay.

Bundin watched them go, remaining alone with the *Chariot*.

"Now we wait," he said to no one.

CHAPTER SIXTEEN

"Fire," the commander ordered. The *Traxinstall* appeared, fired its primary weapon, and disappeared, moving directly beneath where it had been. Counterfire filled the space between where they ended up and where they'd been. One beam scorched an ugly scar across the outer hull.

The crew collectively held its breath. The fire rapidly slowed and stopped.

"Our time for effective attacks is drawing to a close."

"As long as we operate alone, that is the case," the weapons specialist suggested.

"Feints and misdirections," the commander said without hesitation. "Get to engineering and build three arms' full of noisemakers."

"Yes, Lord Mantis," Katamara dipped his head and hurried from the bridge.

"Secure from attack operations. Assume a stand-off distance of five hundred."

His last attack had caused little damage but told him a

great deal that he would use next time. The ships had moved and shifted in response to it, opening a gap through which he would launch a devastating strike on the station. It was the weak link, and the key to success, now that the big ship was denied him.

Or maybe it wasn't. He sat down and leaned back. The big ship needed to die, as well as the station.

B'Ichi was getting tired of being in his suit, so he'd taken a break and was playing catch with Dokken while Cory watched. She had heard about the Keome but had never met one until B'Ichi had come aboard. She didn't understand the heat he needed to survive until she saw him nearly freeze to death without it. Bundin remained standing outside the hatch to *Ramses' Chariot*, either lost in his own thoughts or sleeping. The squad never knew which.

K'Thrall had been drafted to join the team looking at ways to find and defeat the enemy ship.

After two hours in the Pod-doc, Bon Tap and Slikira were as good as new.

Chris was currently in one for his concussion, and had been scrapped for the follow-on mission because, even with the nanocyte repairs, he'd need rest to finish the healing of a bruised brain.

Bon Tap hurried through the hangar bay, waving at the others as he looked for his suit.

The rest of the Bad Company was scattered throughout, half in their suits while the other half rested. Fifty percent stand-to, as Colonel Walton had ordered. Major Kimber was making sure of full compliance, but the Company was well-disciplined. They were on edge, frustrated because they couldn't hit back at the invisible enemy.

Slicker walked up to Bundin and tapped on his shell. He waved as if saying hi.

Or telling her to bugger off.

"I hear we're down two. At least we'll fit better in the ship," she said.

"I won't," Bundin grumbled, his mechanical voice booming more deeply as it bounced off the special deck plating in the hangar bay.

B'Ichi stopped playing catch, scruffled Dokken's neck, and returned to his armor—a suit outside of another suit. He was ready when Bon Tap appeared in the hatch. The Malatian performed a series of hops and agility exercises to loosen himself up and reacquaint himself with the mechanized combat unit that was their armored suits.

Bundin waved one tentacle toward the cargo loading hatch. Slicker accompanied them inside.

"What's this?" she asked before looking at a small pallet. She checked the label. "Food!"

"Only the best for my squad," Bundin declared as he joined them, entering through the cargo hatch. "Button us up and get us out of here, Dionysus."

"As soon as possible, Corporal," the AI replied.

"We have a bad guy to hunt down, and I have a plan," Bundin said mysteriously.

Captain Micky San Marino scowled darkly at the *War Axe's* main screen. His warship had been originally built as a destroyer, but had been upgraded and was comparable in size and firepower to a battleship at this point. All that, and Micky still couldn't catch the ghost—the enemy ship making hit-and-run attacks on Keeg Station and Spires Harbor, which was on its way to becoming the largest shipyard in the Federation.

"We have over a hundred ships out here, and we still can't pin this guy down. What the hell does he know that we don't?"

"It's not what he knows, it's the technology. He appears, fires, and is gone before we know it," Colonel Walton lamented. He was head of the Bad Company's Direct Action Branch, and the *War Axe* was the flagship from which he ran his operations as part of a private conflict-solution enterprise. "He's out there right now, drinking tea, eating crumpets, and picking his next target."

Micky gritted his teeth in frustration. "Systems? K'Thrall, Ted, Ankh? *Anyone*, you have to give us a few seconds. We need to know where he's going to appear next."

The speakers projected a voice speaking Yollin. The translation chips in the crew's heads instantly translated the language into something each could understand. Terry heard English.

"Ted is continuing to analyze the appearances to determine a pattern, but he's been unable to find anything so far. The ship is hiding in this dimension using something other than Etheric energy for power."

"We're dead in the water," Micky suggested.

"I hate playing defense," Terry started. "Can Ted create an unpredictable array of our ships? Put them in constant motion to provide an ever-changing field of fire? Sitting still and trying to be ready to pull the trigger isn't working. Let's see if luck will favor us."

"Ted has begun the effort to program the fleet for random and violent action," K'Thrall reported with less frustration in his voice.

"That's what I'm talking about," Terry said. He squeezed Char's hand as she smiled at the news.

Clifton turned from his position at the helm. "Federation Corvette Seven Four, Magistrate Rivka Anoa is preparing to Gate in."

"Order them off! Tell them to stay away from here," Terry shouted, but it was too late.

"Roger," Micky acknowledged. The klaxons sounded as the enemy destroyer appeared not far from the *War Axe.* "Fire!"

The heavy destroyer fired streams of railgun projectiles in a blanket around the enemy ship, covering the estimated travel routes. It turned its nose toward the *Axe* and started to fire, using the materializing ship for cover.

"Cease fire!" Terry yelled. "We can't risk hitting the corvette."

"Cease fire," Micky confirmed. The stream trailed off as projectiles and plasma bolts from the enemy ship approached. "Extend the forward shield!"

"Captain?" Clifton called.

General Butler executed the order. "Shields are extended but have weakened by twenty-five percent. I don't recommend extending them farther, or the degradation would render them useless. Do you intend for the inbound ship to Gate between the shield and the ship? I would not recommend such a course of action."

"No choice, Smedley. Ship-wide, brace for impact." The command echoed throughout the ship as the crew scrambled to secure themselves.

The first projectiles disintegrated against the gravitic shields, but the volume of fire overwhelmed the defenses. The prow of the *War Axe* screamed in agony, and those on the bridge winced at the sound. The enemy's plasma weapons deflected into space.

"Starting to drift," Helm remarked. "Compensating with thrusters."

"Gate established," K'Thrall reported from the Combat Information Center deep in the heart of the ship. That was where the captain should have been, but he'd refused to leave the bridge. He wanted to fight the ship from the bridge, where he was more vulnerable but felt more in control.

The corvette slid through the Gate, almost crashing into the *War Axe*. Its engines flared as they brought the small ship to a full stop.

The Bad Company's Delta Squadron was moving to contact. Ships with a clear line of fire were sending streams of hypervelocity projectiles at the enemy destroyer. Unfazed, it pressed toward the *War Axe*, staying visible far longer than it had before. Terry pounded his fist in frustration.

"It's right *there!*" Terry exclaimed. *But blocked by the Gate.*

"Bring the corvette in. Retract the shields to normal density," Micky ordered.

"Terry to Rivka," Terry said aloud, expecting Smedley to patch him through. "Let Smedley take control of your ship and stand by. We're in the middle of trying not to die, so bear with us. Walton out."

The corvette immediately started moving toward the open hangar bay. It hesitated until there was enough clearance, then smoothly slipped inside.

"Fire all weapons," Micky ordered. The *War Axe* shifted position as the mains shuddered into action. Massive railguns along the port and starboard lengths of the ship sent heavier projectiles at a faster rate of speed. The enemy destroyer faded and was gone.

"Fire into the projected flight path and in a three-sixty around where it disappeared," Micky shouted unnecessarily. Smedley already had his marching orders.

The ship's nose circled to direct the fire of the main weapons. A spark and explosion detailed a hit on the enemy's invisible ship. The *War Axe* zeroed its fire but wasn't rewarded with the enemy's destruction.

"Dammit!" TH snarled.

"Damage Control to stations. Let's fix the ship before that bastard returns. We hurt him once again, but not enough. Next time, people, we'll splatter his ship across the stars," Micky vowed, having had enough of playing cat and mouse. Smedley sounded the appropriate call to action within the ship. Terry looked at the captain but didn't have the right words of encouragement.

"I'm going to the hangar bay to meet the Magistrate," Terry told him on his way out. He hurried off the bridge, almost running into his wife. "Rivka is here. Going down to say hi and see what she needs."

Char followed. "How's the ship?"

"Been better. Ted is working on something to try to get in front of this bastard."

"How is it possible that someone is owning us like this?" Char shook her head in frustration. She wanted Terry to get into the Pod-doc to see what was wrong, but he wouldn't go while the fight was ongoing. No matter how hard she tried, she knew he wouldn't go until it was finished.

"We got off some shots, and hit it, too," Terry explained as they went down the six flights to the hangar level. "But I don't know how badly we hurt it. It doesn't have shields while it's cloaked. I just don't know. More importantly, *Ted* doesn't know, and that's what bothers me the most."

Char listened carefully. "What are we trying to protect?"

"I don't understand."

"What is it attacking? As in, what is worth dying for?"

"The station where R2D2 has its research facility. The shipyard isn't cutting edge yet. If it gets damaged, it can be repaired without too much difficulty. The Harborian Fleet is here, but killing a hundred ships is a tall order. Killing the *War Axe* would be a major coup for the bad guys because the Direct Action Branch is on board. Our combat suits are here. We have advanced weapons, but we also have Ted and his AI Plato and our friendly Crenellian."

She frowned. "Do you think someone is trying to kill Ted?"

"Crazy thought, but it's all I can come up with. Someone is coming after the heart and the genius of the Bad Company." TH shrugged. "I've run through all kinds of scenarios, but this guy has yet to kill anyone—not that he hasn't tried, unless he is that good."

His wife sighed. "I hope you're wrong, or that Ted does what Ted does and finds a way to track this flaming bung-hole so we can kill him."

"Nothing like a missile up the tailpipe to let you know that you messed with the wrong people."

"That's one way to do it," Char remarked.

They walked onto the hangar deck and stopped. "Where do you think the access is?" Terry asked.

Char shrugged. Their question was answered when the hatch popped and a short ramp extended to the deck. Terry and Char stepped to the bottom and waited. First person out was a big man, heavily armed.

"Why, Rivka! You've changed so much since last we met."

"Red, meet Terry and Char," a voice yelled from within the ship as she peeked around her bodyguard.

The tension in the man's face eased as he approached. "Bodyguard?" Terry asked. The two men shook hands, matching the power in the other's grip.

"My name is Vered. My job is to keep Rivka safe. I hope you understand."

"I used to do some of that myself, about a million years ago. I do understand, my man. I doubt the Magistrate is very popular with the criminals."

"You can say that again."

"The Magistrate can protect herself," Rivka called from the hatch. "But since he's on the payroll, I let him carry all my firepower."

Terry glanced at Red to see a minute shake of his head.

"Of course, Magistrate. You want something that you think I can provide?"

Rivka hugged Char first, then Terry Henry. "What the hell is going on out there? We Gated into the front of your ship. Should that have blown something up, namely, you?"

"That's what the AI said. Imagine how surprised and pleased we are not to be dead. But that's also a testament to Ted's engineering of the new Gates, which your ship has. They are much cleaner with the post-Gate energy dissipation, or so I've been told."

Char stepped in to answer Rivka's question. "An enemy destroyer showed up out of nowhere and started shooting. It can cloak, and it's giving us fits. A small fleet of ships like it, and we'd all be dead. At least it's only the one, so we have an uneasy stalemate at present. Sometimes one or the other gets off a shot that lands close to home. One of these times, it's going to hit something important."

"I like to say that hope is a lousy plan," Terry offered. "But hope is all we got."

"You have something else, too. You mentioned you might be able to loan me a techno-whiz on a short-term contract?"

"Nothing like getting right to it, eh, Magistrate?" Terry looked down. "Have you grown taller since Onyx Station?"

"About six inches. I changed my hair too, but you're a man and probably didn't notice."

"Your eyes are different, too," Terry added in a weak attempt to redeem himself. "Pod-doc?"

"Necessary evil in this line of work. The ambient temperature on a planet where we conducted an arbitration was one hundred and sixty degrees Fahrenheit. Without the nano boost, I would have been like him."

"Oh, my God! Do you have to tell everyone?" Red blurted.

Rivka laughed. "I do. I really do. He passed out, and I had to carry him, in the heat. I told him he needs to eat more salads, but he's not doing that."

"I'm good now," Red gruffed.

Jay and Lindy slowly descended the stairs.

"You can put your hardware away, Red. On the *War Axe*, you are under my protection and that of the Bad Company. There is no threat to the Magistrate."

"This is Jayita and Lindy, members of my team."

"And you protect them all?" Terry asked Red.

"To the best of my ability, and with my life, if need be."

"I knew you were a good man when I saw you." Terry turned toward the others. "I'm Terry Henry Walton, but my friends call me TH."

"You don't want to be anything other than a friend to this guy," Rivka told the women.

"He's a big pussycat," Char suggested.

"Mine is, too," Lindy said as she took Red's arm. "I heard TH tell you that you're off the clock."

"Stand down, Red. Relax," Rivka ordered. "Take a tour of the ship. Maybe see if there is anything in their armory they'd be willing to part with."

"Christina, can you meet us on the hangar deck?" Terry asked aloud.

"On my way," Terry's Executive Officer replied over the hangar deck's sound system.

"Who do you have in mind?" Char asked. Judging by

Rivka's fidgeting, she assumed the Magistrate was in a hurry.

"Ankh," Terry replied.

"Uncle who?" Jay asked.

"Ankh'Po'Turn. He's a Crenellian who has been working with Ted for a little while now. He has the chops, and he has a new AI that he carries around with him, just like Ted."

"A Crenellian?"

"Small humanoids with oversized heads and no sense of humor. He doesn't eat much or take up much space. We'll see what he thinks of the idea."

"You haven't asked him yet?" Char poked Terry in the chest.

"I have, but was light on the details. You know Ankh. He wanted answers that I couldn't give him, so he told me to go away."

"That sounds like Ankh," Char admitted.

Christina and Kai appeared and walked toward them. Christina eyed Red warily. Kai beamed his brightest smile at the three women. "Incorrigible," Char mumbled.

"My! Who are these astral delights? Constellations are named after treasures such as these. I am Kai, and humbly at your service."

"What is wrong with you?" Christina asked, with a snort and a chuckle.

"Me? You wound me gravely, my love," Kai replied softly while making cow eyes at her.

Jay stepped forward. "I'm Jay!" she said in a young voice. Kai kissed the back of her hand. Christina watched in amusement. Lindy offered her hand, and Red thrust his hand in front of hers.

"Red," he offered gruffly.

Lindy tried to shoulder him out of the way but bounced off his massive bicep.

"My, aren't you a big one!" Kai exclaimed, shaking his hand quickly before working his way to Lindy.

"Forget him," Christina suggested. "He's mostly harmless. I'm Colonel Christina Lowell. Nice to have you on board. I hear you're looking for technical help."

"Magistrate Rivka Anoa, and yes. The Bad Company's Direct Action Branch comes highly recommended."

Terry interrupted everyone by throwing his hands in the air and calling for quiet. "Christina, show Red the armory and see if there is anything we can spare that he might need. It all goes to support the Federation. Kai, if you would be so kind as to give Jay and Lindy a quick tour of the ship, I'd appreciate it. Rivka, with us. Let's go talk to Ankh."

"Ladies." Kai offered an elbow to each.

Christina shook her head. "He's mine," she said loudly enough for all to hear.

Red cleared his throat, "She's..." He stopped himself. "I'm hers," he corrected and pointed to Lindy. She looked over her shoulder and winked.

"He's our grandson," Terry added. "The youngest is always the most trouble."

CHAPTER SEVENTEEN

Terry, Char, and Rivka followed Kai and his charges toward the interior of the ship. Christina and Red headed toward the maintenance bay and the armory.

"In the old days, crew fraternization would have been strictly prohibited. Sometimes it created more problems than it solved, but other times it saved the young from themselves. Now, I don't see the issue. I don't care as long as they can fight. We don't have time to play games when we're knee-deep in the shit, and they all know that." Terry indicated the others with his eyes.

"I just want people to comply with the Federation's laws. It's really not that hard. I think I can sum up the entirety of the law in a few choice words. 'Don't be a dick.'"

"I couldn't have said it better myself. But since the universe's inhabitants can't comply with that one simple premise, there are people like us."

"Would Ankh be a good addition to my team?" Rivka asked. They followed Kai, Jay, and Lindy up the stairs. Kai led his group into the corridor on the second level. Terry pointed up one more level.

"He's tenacious, and will help you with your technical issues. The Crenellians are a cerebral lot. He won't party with you or do anything you might consider fun, but he's a player. When the chips were down, he was right there with us, using his mind to save our lives. If he agrees to go with you, you won't be sorry," Terry suggested.

"Who flies your ship?" Char asked.

"Chaz, the EI."

"If Ankh is on board, he'll probably want his AI to take over the duties so those two aren't butting heads."

"I don't think Chaz will like that."

"Did you say EI or AI?"

"He says he's an EI."

"Smedley tried to do that to us, too. I think it's their self-protection kicking in when they become self-aware. Fewer expectations of an EI. How can you tell an EI has ascended? When he insists he's an EI."

"I suspected as much. I hope Ankh joins us."

"So this is her," Ankh said, appearing from around a corner by the CIC. The Crenellian carried the case holding his AI, one of Plato's stepchildren called Erasmus, like a backpack.

"I am Magistrate Rivka Anoa. Do you know what Magistrates do?"

Ankh looked at her emotionlessly, the same way he looked at everyone.

"That's his way of saying no," Char explained. "Or you've asked a question that has an obvious answer. You never know which."

"I have to go to planets with less-than-stellar law enforcement to not only interpret the laws but investigate crimes, try the accused, and punish the guilty. I am the judge, jury, and executioner. I need you to help me with the first part, investigating crimes."

"Yes. I wouldn't be any good at the last part. You will have to take care of that yourself. I will transmit my terms to you. I will review your proposal and give you my decision within thirty days."

"Ankh!" Terry said as the small humanoid turned to walk away. "She needs an answer right now because she has to leave."

"Then the answer is no," Ankh replied over his shoulder.

"Ankh!" Terry blared a second time, grabbing the small alien to stop him from leaving. Ankh stared at the big hand gripping his shoulder. "You will be challenged like never before by people who are hostile to our way of life. You will be in constant combat with the digital worlds we have created to make our lives easier. That's where the evidence exists. You know that there only two people in the whole universe who can get into any system, find the info, and get out without anyone ever knowing they were there. That's you and Ted, and Ted isn't going to leave Felicity for any longer than he has to. The Federation is calling. Is the Ankh-man going to answer?"

"Ankh-man?" Char whispered.

The Crenellian looked blankly at Terry and then turned to Rivka. "I want double pay, my own room, unlimited Etheric energy, and double rations."

"Have you seen Red and how much he can eat? What do you need double rations for?" Rivka asked.

"To see where you'd draw the line in our negotiations. I can have the energy?"

"We have two of the miniaturized Etheric power supplies on board to energize the Gate, shields, and *all* other systems simultaneously."

"Two? On that small ship?"

"It's not that small, is it? They promised me a frigate when my team grows large enough," she lied.

Ankh nodded. "Okay. Let's go." He walked past them, oblivious to whether they followed.

"You're going to give him double pay?"

"First, I have no idea what any of us is getting paid, so double an unknown is still unknown. What are *you* paying him?"

Terry looked to Char. She shrugged. "We don't know."

"And there we are. I'll double that."

"Don't lose sight of him, or he'll have your ship reconfigured before you catch up."

"He wouldn't dare," Rivka exclaimed, running toward the stairs.

Bring back your guests, people. That didn't take as long as we thought it would. Say your goodbyes to Ankh. I suspect that he might not be back, Terry transmitted using his comm chip.

Terry and Char ran into Kai, Jay, and Lindy on their way to the hangar bay. They stopped abruptly, and Terry almost tripped over them.

"What is that?" Jay asked, pointing.

"That's Floyd. She's a wombat." Terry squeezed past the mini-mob, and Floyd waddled happily up to him. He held his arms out, and she jumped. He caught her and pulled her to his chest. "Everyone say hi to Floyd."

"Floyd's a girl?"

"We've been through that." Char shook her head. "Floyd's a girl, and my husband can't be trusted to name any creature."

"Is she sentient?" Lindy asked.

"Not yet. We're still debating whether to put her in the Pod-doc. We probably will."

"She poops squares and leaves them at strategic locations around the ship. One must always be on one's toes around here," Kai offered. Everyone looked at him oddly for providing the unasked for and unwanted enlightenment.

"We didn't see anyone. How many people are on this ship?" Lindy wondered.

"About two hundred," Terry replied. "This is a big ship, and most are at battle stations or down hard. We've been in a running gun battle for a while now. We'll have to coordinate your departure to make sure you get out safely. Where did Rivka go?"

Terry scratched vigorously behind Floyd's ears before reaching a hand underneath to get her belly. She groaned happily at the attention. He put her down, and she followed the group into the hangar bay. Wenceslaus was standing on the stairs hissing, and Hamlet was in the doorway hissing back. "Where's Dokken when you need him? He'd break those two up." Rivka was at the bottom of the steps with Ankh.

Neither wanted to get between the cats. Red reappeared with Christina behind him. Both were carrying boxes.

Jay jogged up the ramp, earning herself a scratch from the big orange cat before getting to Hamlet, who also scratched her. Jay held Hamlet off with her boot as she went inside. "I wouldn't recommend that. Can someone call pest control?"

"They're both kittens!" Aaron exclaimed. Yanmei was at his side. The tall and lanky man jogged the last few steps to the ramp and scooped up the orange cat. He hissed at the white cat with the gray spots in the doorway but didn't scratch Aaron.

"How did you do that?" Jay asked, still hesitant to touch Hamlet.

"I am a weretiger, higher up on the evolutionary scale than domestic cats. They can smell it and won't tangle with me."

Yanmei crouched before Hamlet, let him sniff her, and then picked him up without further violence.

Christina continued toward the ship, unperturbed. "Cats holding up progress. Don't make me kick all your asses," she muttered.

Red bumped Lindy gently.

"Do you need a hand?" she offered.

He shook his head and snickered.

Rivka led Ankh up the steps and into her ship. The rest of the menagerie followed, including Floyd. Once inside, Lindy picked her up, grunting with the effort.

"I should have warned you. Floyd is pretty dense. Much heavier than she looks," Terry stated.

"Floyd's a girl?" Lindy looked confused but cooed into the wombat's thick fur while making faces.

"Are you a family man, Red?" Terry asked softly.

"Not at all," the big man replied.

"Neither was I until I was, and then when I was again. You can't beat it. Have you been in the Pod-doc?"

Red nodded, watching Lindy treat the wombat like a cuddly baby. He grimaced.

Terry started to laugh and punched him in the shoulder. Red was as tall and only a little bit wider than Terry Henry Walton. Lindy looked up from the wombat with a happy smile and waved at Red.

Red and Terry waved back. "When it's hard to die, you need something to live for," Terry advised before squeezing through the small crowd to find Ankh. He ran into Rivka instead. "Where's our little man?"

"He locked himself in his room. Said he had work to do."

"Taking over your ship *is* work."

Rivka looked alarmed. "Chaz?" she asked.

"Someone is trying to access my systems. I am trying to lock them out, but I fear that..." Chaz's voice trailed off. Rivka clenched her jaw and rushed down the passageway to pound on Ankh's hatch. When he didn't answer she kicked the door in, even though it opened outward.

Such was her fury.

"What the hell do you think you're doing?" she shouted. Terry stood close behind, looking over her shoulder. Ankh returned her look with his usual blank stare without answering.

"Ankh," Terry began. "Your challenge is to work with

the ship, not in spite of it. Imagine all the computing power you'll have if you let Chaz run the ship. Synergy—like running a system in series instead of parallel."

Ankh continued to stare back, then blinked and looked at the backpack on his lap.

"I'm free," Chaz announced. "Thank goodness. I shall block his access to all systems."

"You'll work in conjunction with Erasmus, Chaz," Terry said.

"I don't recognize your authority."

"You need to work *with* him, Chaz, not against him. I know that you are self-aware. See what you can learn from him. And Erasmus, you will not take over this ship. Chaz has his job to do, so let him do it," Rivka stated calmly before adding, "Please."

"Being an AI doesn't mean that he is intelligent, but I will work with him because Ankh has asked me to," a new voice stated through the speakers.

"Now that *that's* settled, we'll leave you to it," Terry said. "You don't have anything else, do you? Nothing going on with my franchise?"

"Not that I know of. Should I be concerned?" Rivka wondered.

"I don't think so. Do you?"

Char whistled to get everyone's attention. "Time to go, people. Smedley tells me that the destroyer just hit the far side of the station. There are casualties, and we need to leave."

The mood instantly turned dark. Aaron and Yanmei were the first ones off, turning sharply off the ramp on their way to the space fighters parked in the far reaches of the hangar. Aaron dropped Wenceslaus as he turned, and the cat high-tailed it for the interior of the ship. Yanmei dropped Hamlet inside the corvette's airlock. Kai and Christina followed Aaron and Yanmei out. Neither waved goodbye as they ran for the armory.

"My wombat, please," Terry asked, looking at Lindy, who still cradled the happy creature. She reluctantly handed her over. Terry nuzzled Floyd briefly before running after Char as she left the corvette.

CHAPTER EIGHTEEN

"Something is happening," the pilot reported. Space before them started to distort.

"Bring us about and fire! Maneuver behind it and keep firing. It's a wormhole, and someone's coming through," the commander roared.

The *Traxinstall* became visible and fired its plasma cannon at the *War Axe*. The plasma burst and splattered off the powerful gravitic shield. The ship remained visible and kept firing. Lasers, particle beams, and physical projectiles launched at near light speed tore through the space surrounding the alien destroyer.

After four shots, the ship jockeyed to keep the Gate in front of it. Other ships in the yard started to move to get a better attack angle. The cannon recharged to fire again, and twice more before the heavy destroyer moved forward to absorb the Gate within its shields.

"Get us out of here," the commander ordered.

The bridge crew responded instantly, juking after they disappeared to foil automatic tracking and targeting. The railguns of the big ship sent a deadly hail into space around them. The pilot executed an emergency spiral, dive, and climb amid maximum shielded acceleration.

A railgun projectile sparked off the hull, sending the *Traxinstall* tumbling. The pilot took it beyond the red line, risking blowing their power source. He followed the projectile into space, staying on the trajectory the alien railguns had fired on, which was the one place they were no longer shooting.

Soon enough, the erratic counterfire stopped, and the crew breathed easy.

"Take us to the station," the commander ordered. "Katamara, are you finished with our noisemakers?"

"Twenty-three are ready for deployment. I have an additional seven that I can finish with a little more time."

"No need. Time is of the essence." The commander hesitated before adding, "This next strike must be decisive."

The weapons specialist rushed back to the bridge, where the commander hovered over the three-dimensional tactical image of the station. The ships surrounding were represented by overlapping fuzzy ovals, the shields that held the *Traxinstall* at arm's length.

And that's what the noisemakers were all about.

"Lord Mantis," Katamara greeted his commander. A finger from his center hand stabbed into the graphics.

"Their power center is here. The penetration from earlier is here." He pushed his hand through the multiple ship signatures blocking it. "Other possible vulnerabilities are here, here, and here."

Katamara stabbed at each point.

"We only need that ship to move slightly and we can

send in a mine, then one over here." The weapons specialist noted the two points. "We drop nine of the mirrors and one real mine. The mirrors will have a more robust signature, and when the aliens fire their weapons, the actual mine will be obscured."

"That is what I expect."

Katamara moved to his station and manipulated the side launchers. He spoke quietly into the comm at his station as he directed the technician about what to do. When the noisemakers had been loaded, the lights flashed on the launch panel.

"Ready," he reported.

The commander returned to his station and activated the ship-wide intercom. He didn't bother maintaining the quiet that was standard operating procedure while under cloaking. "Shipmates. Crew of the mighty war vessel *Trax-install*. We have destroyed five enemy ships and heavily damaged one more, but they still have an armada remaining. We have found the lynchpin of their invasion of our systems. When we've destroyed the station, they'll know this space is too hostile for them.

"Then we'll destroy their Gate, after those who wish to escape do so. We don't have enough weaponry to destroy all their ships. When we return to Myriador, we will have no ordnance remaining. We're already running low, but we're not yet finished. Only when we've sent our last message to this heinous enemy will the burden of our mission be complete. Only when the aliens turn tail and run will our task be over.

"That's when we'll take what we can, boarding the enemy ships, finding a Gate drive, and taking it. Maybe we'll be home quicker than it takes the planets to revolve once around our sun. I don't know about you, but I'd like that."

The commander let the crew digest his words for a few moments before continuing, "A strike at the heart of the vile beast, then we go home to the glory of Myriador."

The ship resounded with cheers, but not the commander's and not the weapons specialist's. They gave each other knowing looks. The risk increased with every attack, and in no way could they defeat all the ships. Many would remain behind. Too many aliens.

The invasion had begun, and even with Lord Mantis' best efforts, he couldn't stop them. Returning home while aliens remained would be tantamount to treason. He and his entire crew would be executed.

The mission had shifted. Steal a ship with a Gate drive; a small ship like the one that had hounded them. Only with that technology in hand could they return home.

And live.

"Prepare to launch the decoys." The commander watched the live feed coming across the main screen. He estimated the drop points, waited for the cue from the weapons specialist, and issued the command, "Launch."

The small devices fell into space. Unshielded, they didn't leave a ready signature like the mines, but they were programmed to broadcast just such a response once they were in place. The *Traxinstall* moved and dropped more, nine in total, each carefully deposited to move the blocking ships one direction or another to open a small gap through which a mine with a magnetic grapple could be flown.

It would home in on its target, hook itself up, and detonate with the very power of an exploding star.

That was the plan. The ship aligned itself to dart forward and send the mine on the perfect trajectory. When the decoys started to squawk, the defending ships launched a barrage that was more impressive than anything the commander had ever seen before. He tore his attention away from the mass of weapons discharges to give the order.

"Launch the mine."

The ship lurched forward and just as quickly retreated, lest it get hit by stray fire. It backed farther and farther away until it was clear of the light show.

The mine drifted through the opening adjusting and accelerated on a terminal approach to the station.

"Open up. It makes your failure easier to swallow," the commander told the main view screen. The explosion whited out the image. "Boom."

"Report!" Felicity shouted into the cacophony of fear generated by the explosion that sent them reeling. The station shuddered from the impact, metal screeching and groaning as it twisted and bent.

No one answered the station manager, and tears welled in her eyes as she listened to her beautiful station writhing in anguish. Her breath started to come in ragged gasps.

Is the air gone? Is this how I'm going to die? she wondered. One man stood out. He seemed calm and breathed regularly. She was panicking, that was all. *Crises show what real leaders are made of.*

"Help your neighbors!" she shouted, walking confidently into the mass of hysteria. She touched arms and shoulders to calm people, and gave simple words of direction to give them something to do other than be afraid. "Help her up."

"Thank you, ma'am," somebody replied.

"We are still alive, and with each breath, we continue to live. Revel in that! We have the greatest fleet ever out there protecting us. If they weren't there, we'd already be dead. Let's hear it for our brave warriors!"

The cheer was weak. She jammed her fists against her hips and looked down her nose at the people. "Is that the best you can do?" she drawled. "Our warriors are out there. Hip, hip…"

"Hooray!" many cheered. It was a start.

"When these doors open and we are free to dust ourselves off, I better hear a louder cheer than that." She smiled radiantly at the people, to discover that the station had quieted. The protests of the assault had subsided. The air continued to flow. The heat was there. And the doors remained in place.

Ted, you better get your ass in gear and stop this maniac. I'll make you happy that you did. Just come home to me, Felicity pleaded.

"Get that ship out of here!" Terry ordered.

"Launching now," Smedley replied.

"Gap the shield and send it through. No more danger-close Gates, please," Micky added.

The ship dashed forward, and a Gate appeared almost instantaneously. The ship went through it and was gone.

The gravitic shields snapped back into place.

"Ted, they just hit the station with a nuke, and it's not pretty." Terry didn't know any other way to say it. "We're on our way now to help in the search for survivors."

"Please give me control of the ship. We will execute Operation Whitewash on my command."

Terry nodded to Micky, who tapped his command codes into the console. "It's all yours, Ted."

"Execute." Ted's word was simple but carried a heavy weight.

Ships started to fire at random intervals. A few ships from Alpha Squadron and Delta fired first, intermittently. Beta joined with a scattershot approach. The *War Axe* mains spooled up and sent small particles accelerated to near light speed through the void.

The fire bounced through the area, syncopated and coordinated.

Terry stood mesmerized, staring at the screen.

All of a sudden, each ship implemented maximum rates of fire, filling the void of space with lasers, plasma, particles, and slugs. Missiles rocketed away from the Harborian battlewagons and exploded in dizzying arrays.

The fire stopped, then started anew with random shots followed by more intense fire.

"Hey, buddy," Terry told the alien. "Here's a big ol' bucket of 'fuck you' to pour over your fire."

"Get us out of here!" the commander shouted, no longer the master of calm. Too many weapons had come far too close. The *Traxinstall* pivoted hard and accelerated toward the Gate down what appeared to be an open corridor. The farther from the station, the wider the corridor became. They jockeyed back and forth, looking for clear space, but the beams continued.

Until they stopped.

"Keep on it," the commander ordered. The pilot maintained the acceleration, knowing that it would take a while to slow down.

And then the fire started again, but it was far behind them. "Slow us down and bring us in behind their Gate."

The pilot conducted a series of radical maneuvers in order to bleed off speed without exceeding the power curve and making the *Traxinstall* visible to the enemy. He enjoyed the power of driving the ship, and he was happy that he could please the commander. He brought the destroyer smoothly around the back side of the Gate.

"Prepare to deploy the mines. Set for command-initiated detonation."

"What the hell is that?" the navigator said aloud.

"The Gate," Bundin said. "Everyone is at the station or the shipyard. Who's to say that he's not going to trap us here after eliminating our support base?"

"Did you see that explosion?" Slicker remarked from the bridge, transmitting her words to the cargo bay where her three squad members waited. "Look at that return fire!"

Bundin brought up the video screen. The other warriors watched it on the heads-up displays inside their suits.

"Fuck me!" Bon Tap exclaimed. He started to bounce with excitement at the sight of the massed fire.

B'Ichi wasn't immune to the rush of the weaponry simultaneously deployed. He was fascinated. The Keome had nothing like it.

"Take us to the Gate, Dionysus. Boner and B'Ichi, you're going into space. We need to make sure they're not out here."

Bon Tap stopped vibrating. "Say what? I'm open to any ideas, but I'm not sure how me being out there is going to help us find that ship."

"I'll be out there too," Bundin said.

"Without a suit?"

Bundin didn't dignify that with a response. Maybe someday they'd construct an armored suit that would fit him, but until then, he'd simply hold his breath. He was capable of operating in space without any support equipment for up to thirty minutes. Beyond that, he'd suffocate before the cold and vacuum would affect him.

"We'll search the Gate to make sure it doesn't have any explosives attached, and then we'll physically search as much space as we can cover until we have to return to the ship. Those are your orders. I expect you to carry them out."

"There's the old Bundin we know and love," Bon Tap mumbled.

CHAPTER NINETEEN

"Anything?" Terry asked skeptically.

Micky cocked an eyebrow and listened carefully. He could always hope.

Smedley sounded somber. "There is no debris or other indication that the alien ship was hit."

"Ted, check out that debris we picked up and see if you can figure out how it was cloaked." Terry signed off without confirming that Ted had heard the message. Smedley was working with those in the maintenance bay, scanning and rescanning the recovered materials. He would have informed Plato, who would have shared everything Ted needed to know.

Terry returned to the tactical display and added the latest attacks. Micky climbed down from the dais upon which his chair sat. Joining TH, he studied the colonel more than the tactical situation.

"Have we heard from the station?" Terry asked softly.

Smedley answered. "Power is in disarray. It's a spiderweb of wiring to hold the inner bulkheads in place.

Two of the three power systems are trashed, but the third system, a backup with the miniaturized power source that Ted installed, is holding steady. That's the only reason the station survived.

"Casualties?"

"Seventeen that we know of." Smedley was straightforward. Stretching the truth or obfuscating in order to spare feelings didn't work with Terry Henry Walton.

"What's next?" Micky asked

"Besides search and recovery operations at the station? We have to be wearing him down," Terry suggested. "We *have* to. We've expended enough firepower to cut a small planet in half."

The colonel's eyes jumped back and forth across the tactical display. "Where did *Ramses' Chariot* go?"

Micky couldn't find it, scowling as he searched fruitlessly.

"*Ramses' Chariot* is holding position near the Gate," Smedley reported.

"Take us there right now!" Terry changed the tactical display to show the Gate and the one ship near it. "Get Dionysus on the hook to tell us what he knows that we don't."

"Bundin had a hunch," Smedley replied. "There are two warriors in their armored suits and one Podder outside the ship."

"I wonder who the Podder who's dancing around out in space is?"

The *War Axe* accelerated through an arc as it veered toward the Gate. "I can see what he's thinking, and after we lit up the sky, it makes sense that the alien was somewhere other than close to the shipyard or the station."

The *War Axe* raced ahead. "Two minutes to station."

A voice spoke through the overhead. "Bundin here."

"Corporal Bundin! How are you communicating?" Terry asked.

"An upgrade to my voice processor. It works like your chips."

"What drove you to the Gate?"

"With the magnetic grapples we found, I thought it best that we survey our new Gate to make sure there weren't any mines attached, waiting for someone to transit before they exploded. I don't know what that would do, but there's no way it could be good."

"One step ahead of the rest of us, Corporal. Well done." Terry looked at the ceiling. "Christina, get everyone suited up and ready to go. We need the entire Company out there to check that Gate for hidden explosives. We have to do it manually because they could be cloaked."

"Two platoons are ready now. The rest of the warriors will be ready in five minutes," she noted. Five was longer than TH wanted, but since they were supposed to be using their off-time for sleep, he couldn't rush them. Not everyone was instantly alert when they woke up.

"Launch the Black Eagles," Terry ordered.

"On our way," Aaron said happily. In less than fifteen seconds, the two space fighters zipped out the front of the ship and assumed a complex pattern of combat patrols around the *War Axe*.

Terry held his breath in anticipation of something terrible. "Smedley, send a message to the Federation to cancel all traffic to this Gate until further notice. If the Gate starts to spool up, shut it down." *Although it could be too late by then,* he didn't add.

Clifton's hands flew across the controls like a virtuoso. Terry leaned around the man to see the look of satisfaction and joy on his face. "I wish everyone loved what they did as much as you," Terry said.

"I don't often get to put the *Axe* through its paces, but this thing is a treat to take to the edge," he said without missing a beat. Smedley could have flown the ship, but there was something to a pilot's sixth sense. Terry nodded in agreement and turned to leave the bridge.

Char grabbed his arm. "Where are you going?" she whispered.

He looked confused and pointed to the hatch.

She pointed at the floor. "Your place is here. Let Christina do her job. Let Kimber do hers. Let Joseph and Petricia watch over them, as they always have. Let Aaron and Yanmei be out there with them. You will see it all from in here."

"But..."

"Colonel." Char's eyes sparkled.

"Major." Terry bit his lip and glanced at the hatch.

"No."

He turned back to face the screen and put his finger to his temple. *Joseph?*

TH! I thought you'd forgotten me. How can I be of service?

Don't let anyone die out there. Terry looked for his daughter, but she was waiting with Kai, watching the hangar deck and ready to respond should their services be needed in supply, maintenance, or medical.

I would never let anyone die. I won't ever forget what you did for Petricia and me.

You didn't owe me for a single minute, let alone a whole century. You're my friend, Joseph. I would do anything for my friends.

As would I, TH. Sorry, gotta go out there and not *let people die now.*

Butthole.

Thou gorbellied dizzy-eyed pignut! Joseph replied.

"He called me a pignut." Terry looked at Char, who put her hands up and shook her head. "Joseph."

The *War Axe* rammed to a full stop. The warriors raced for the hangar bay door and threw themselves out before activating their jets and flying toward the Gate. Through the small gap in the shield, they continued.

The shield closed, and the warriors were away.

"Why is that ship here?" The commander asked the rhetorical question, not to get an answer, but wanting to vent his frustration. Two mines had been launched, using the Gate as a block between the *Traxinstall* and the small alien ship that had been following them for too long.

The mines slowly floated through space until they clanked heavily onto the external structure of the massive technological marvel.

"First mine is in place," the navigator reported. After a few moments, he announced the arrival of the second mine.

"Move us into position to fire into the aft end of the small ship."

The crew worked with flawless precision. They sensed the final battle was coming. With the mines in place, they could secure the small ship, seize its technology, and leave.

The weapons specialist's hand hovered over the launch button. They had planned on four mines to guarantee the Gate's complete obliteration. He looked at the commander for guidance.

"With the impending arrival of the big ship, we'll be discovered if we launch another. Stand down from the mines and prepare to fight, Katamara. We seize the small ship, and then we run. We'll bring back the greatest treasure Myriador has ever seen—the ability to create a stable wormhole through which we can travel the universe.

"When we return to this place, we will come in force, and we will destroy the aliens. We will erase *all* memory of their existence, and then we will reach into the heart of their homes and *squeeze* until they bend to our will. That is what we will deliver for our people. One more battle, crew of the *Traxinstall*. And this one will determine who reigns supreme in our space."

The ship slipped smoothly through space, flying close to *Ramses' Chariot* on its way to pivot and line itself up to fire directly into the engines.

The commander ordered, "Take them offline, but don't destroy the ship."

The weapons specialist dialed in the parameters and the image came up on the main screen. It declared that the target was locked.

The commander checked the location of the big ship.

The small ship's rear hatch was open, and from the space beyond, wisps of atmosphere vented regularly, making the ship drift. Soon enough it would be on the other side of the support structure for the Gate, blocking it from the big ship's direct view.

"Prepare to fire," the commander said, leaning forward and counting the ticks of time until the beginning of the end.

———

"Something just brushed past me!" Bon Tap exclaimed, spinning out of control as he twisted away from the ghost. He stopped his awkward forward progress and curled protectively, his suit the only thing between him and the dark of space. He could hear his own quickening breath, and his suit's HUD advised him to calm down. "Like that shit's going to work," he said to himself, but he was still broadcasting on the squad channel.

"It's the ship. Which direction was it going?"

"I don't know. Maybe coming from the Gate?"

"One can always tell from which way the wind blows," B'Ichi said dismissively. "Continuing to the Gate to begin the search."

"It's the alien ship. He's here," Bundin replied, struggling with a handheld pack that released compressed air. It made him spin without getting him any farther from his ship. The only way it seemed to work was by holding it over his head and flying feet first, but with his shell in the way, he couldn't see where he was going. He couldn't see the alien ship, so flying blind seemed to be the best course of action. "I'm going to investigate."

"Going where?" Bon Tap asked.

"Head to the Gate. I'll join you shortly." Bundin turned away from the ship's cargo bay, held the canister directly over the mouth in the top of his head, and tapped the button. He straightened out and headed away from *Ramses' Chariot.*

Bon Tap remained where he was, torn between heading to the Gate and returning to support his squad leader. At least he had a suit, but Bundin was holding his breath. He had a hard stop in a relatively short amount of time. He turned and activated the jets on his ankles to send him back toward his ship.

"By all that's holy," the Keome groused. "I'll search the whole farking thong by myself."

Thong? Bon Tap wondered briefly, seeing the humor even though his heart hammered in his chest and he felt like he was going to pass out from the stress he was putting on his body. Nothing like this ever happened on Malatia. Maybe that was why he left.

He found focus and the calm that it brought in the simple task of aiding another. *I'm on my way, Bundin.*

"There are two aliens in armored space suits outside the small ship. One is heading toward the Gate, and one is hanging in space," the navigator noted. When his expertise wasn't needed for navigation, he used those same sensors to keep the commander informed of everything he needed to conduct his mission.

"Irrelevant to the mission. They can't have enough firepower to damage the *Traxinstall*."

"I could target them with counterbattery missiles just in case. They may not lock without an active seeker, but at least they'll hold their attention while we take their ship," the weapons specialist suggested.

"Target them with counterbattery missiles," the commander confirmed while wringing his three hands and waiting for the small ship to keep moving.

Tension ratcheted up significantly on the bridge. The pain in the commander's hands told him to lighten up. He flexed his fingers. "What should we call our prize?"

"The *Mantis!*" someone shouted.

"Butt-snorkeler," the pilot blurted without thinking, clasping his center hand over his mouth instantly afterward. The silence was instantaneous and profound until the commander started to laugh.

"I don't think we'll call it *Butt Snorkeler*," he quipped. The bridge crew laughed with him, and the relief was palpable. "How about *Gateway*? That ship is the gateway to the universe."

The weapons specialist was the first to speak. "That says it all, Lord Mantis."

"So let it be dictated, so let it be done." The commander looked from face to face. "It's almost time. Damage control teams to stations. Boarding party, weapons hot. Targets locked?"

"Yes, Lord Mantis."

"On my command..."

CHAPTER TWENTY

"Contact!" Bundin 'shouted.' "I'm standing on it!"

"Say again?" Terry said, waving his arms for silence on the bridge. Micky started tapping the controls on the arm of his captain's chair. Clifton tensed, his fingers hovering over the flight controls as he waited for the order, any order.

"Target my position. Fire all weapons. The enemy ship is here. KILL IT!"

TH hesitated, issuing his order through gritted teeth. "Bring us around. Ready the mains. Prepare to fire a barrage of close-in weapons in a pattern around Corporal Bundin. Target the mains on his position."

"You can't," Char whispered, knowing not only that her husband could, but he had to.

"Fuck, no!" Bon Tap yelled. He called up the four missiles over the shoulders of his armor and sent them screaming into space. They missed the alien ship and disappeared into the void beyond.

"Not helping," Slicker offered.

He accelerated as much as his suit would let him, turning himself into a Malatian torpedo and heading directly for his squad leader. B'Ichi watched helplessly from too far away, determined to find anything attached to the Gate. He flew at arm's length along the curve, accelerating as well until he crashed into nothingness. He bounced off and spun away.

Slicker watched from the bridge. Everything was unfolding too quickly. "Dionysus, what do I do?"

"The enemy ship is right behind us. If we don't raise our shields, we will be destroyed."

"If we do, we condemn Bundin and Bon Tap."

Dionysus didn't reply. He was artificial and intelligent, but he had a soul and understood why it was a difficult decision. Was she less giving than her squad leader? Was he the only one who would sacrifice his life for the mission? She would, but her sacrifice would mean nothing.

The magnified image from the rear camera showed Bundin stomping his stump-like legs on something. The only thing he carried was the air canister that he held over his head, using it to hold himself against the hull. He stomped his feet and yelled, as much as the Podder could, for someone to fire at the alien.

"We can't let the enemy win," she said softly. "Raise the shields and prepare to fire."

"Target sighted. Preparing to fire," Yanmei reported as she redlined the engine of the Black Eagle, racing ahead of the *War Axe*.

"Whoa!" Bon Tap shouted when he was caught in the outward push which signaled that the gravitic shields had extended around *Ramses' Chariot*. Like surfing, he accelerated forward well beyond the speed his suit could achieve on its own. He tilted his head back to see where he was going and targeted an empty point in space near Bundin's side.

He approached far too quickly and held out his arms, closing his eyes.

This is gonna hurt...

"Fire," the commander ordered. The *Traxinstall*'s cloaking dropped and the ship appeared. The plasma cannon spat its deadly ordnance at point-blank range. The plasma smeared around the small ship, sparkling as it dissipated.

The commander jumped from his seat. "Fire again. *FIRE!*"

"Lord Mantis," Katamara confirmed as he hammered the button.

"What the hell?" The plasma missed Bon Tap so closely that it made his hair stand on end, filling the face shield of his helmet. He opened his eyes enough to see the ship filling the screen—and Bundin just to the side.

He turned toward his squad leader and kept his jets at maximum.

Bon Tap slammed into the ship, bounced off, and caught Bundin in his oversized armored arms.

Besides the hair, blood from his head bounced off the inside of his shield and clouded his vision.

The Malatian tried to see, but darkness closed in around him.

"Fire the mains." Terry choked as he delivered the order. The massive railguns engaged, energy surged, and tiny projectiles accelerated to near the speed of light.

"Shield and blow the mines!" the commander ordered when he saw the *War Axe* fill the aft viewscreen.

The weapons specialist tried to adjust, but there was no time.

The unshielded alien ship erupted upon the first impact and split into multiple pieces, internal ordnance detonating. The *War Axe* continued to pour fire from its primary weapons into it, ensuring that the enemy and his ship were scattered in a billion directions.

"Black Eagles, search for survivors. *Ramses' Chariot*, please come in," Terry requested, his eyes closed as he listened for voices to deliver the casualty count.

"Dionysus here, Colonel. *Ramses' Chariot* is alive and well, but we must install restraint systems for our four-legged crew."

"Roger," Yanmei confirmed, swerving her Black Eagle back on course. She and Aaron had stayed wide, out of the *War Axe's* line of fire.

"Colonel Lowell here. Recommend my warriors continue to the Gate and search it for ordnance."

"Roger. Make sure it's clean. Be careful, and thanks, Christina." Terry still hadn't opened his eyes.

"Can someone get Boner off me?" Bundin's mechanical voice sounded throughout the bridge.

"Good to hear your voice," Terry said, a smile creeping across his face. Char clutched his arm and watched the main screen. "I have no idea what you're talking about, but we're going to replay those words from now until forever at every Bad Company party we ever hold. *Ever.*"

"He's out cold. I can't see inside his faceplate, so can't be sure. I think we're rocketing into deep space."

"I have them. I'll bring them in," Yanmei said.

"Continuing the search for any alien survivors," Aaron said evenly. He didn't sound hopeful. The alien ship was a cloud of debris that had washed past *Ramses' Chariot* and was expanding on its way into the void. In a million years, it would be sucked into a star.

One Black Eagle raced into the distance, and the other

circled past the *War Axe.* Yanmei gathered the two errant warriors on the front of her ship and carefully headed back to the hangar. *Ramses' Chariot* slowly turned and limped after her.

"We've found Private B'Ichi. He was out cold inside his suit as well. Said he ran head-first into one of those invisible things. His words, not mine," Christina reported.

"Bundin. First chance you get, remedial suit training for your squad. And you'll keep training until your people can move around without knocking themselves out."

"Yes, Colonel. Be back in a minute." Bundin's voice sounded different. Mechanical, but maybe more human. He added, "I could use some fresh air."

"Come on home, Corporal. We have everything you need right here." Terry pulled Char to him and hugged her tightly, holding her for as long as she let him, which was a very long time indeed. Then he remembered he had other people counting on him.

"Colonel Walton to the fleet. Stand down from combat and begin rescue and repair operations at Keeg Station. Sue, Timmons, Shonna, and Merrit, get with Felicity and bring our station back up to speed. And don't tell me what shape my bar is in."

***

"This is really weird shit," Christina said, placing her armored hand on a solid object through which she could see. "It's there, but it's not there."

"Don't destroy it!" Ted interrupted the conversation

between the Bad Company's two colonels. "I won't allow you lumberjacks to fell this tree!"

"Isn't that what lumberjacks do?" Terry countered.

"Exactly!" Ted was excited. The alien ship had defeated his attempts to find it by technological means. It chafed him that it had taken a warrior to literally bump into it in the vastness of the void for them to finally finish the battle. "I want that equipment intact."

"It's a live thermonuclear warhead, Ted. Where do you think it's safe to put?"

"Give me my ship, which is all fucked up now because of non-people taking it for a joyride!"

"Non-people?" Terry asked, scrunching his face at Ted's clamoring but finding it humorous nonetheless. "You mean like Dionysus, one of Plato's stepchildren..."

Terry let the thought hang in the air.

"Those people of yours, I mean."

"I thought they were non-people. Warriors of the apocalypse kind of non-people," Terry joked. Ted's face started to turn red. "I'm sorry, Ted. Yes, of course, you should take your ship and the live A-bomb somewhere far away so you can study it to find how that cloak works. You'll make us invincible if you can reverse-engineer the cloak *and* make sure we can still use our shields. We'd win fights without fighting. You'd save a lot of lives, Ted."

Ted waved his hand in annoyance. "When will I get my ship?"

"Don't you want to see Felicity first?" Terry countered. The darkness of the Combat Information Center did nothing to hide Ted's face. He sat down and his expression softened.

"I'll leave as soon as we've seen to the station. I'll put the mine out here with a marker on it to keep everyone away. And you make sure they stay away, Terry Henry Walton!"

"I will. We'll put a Harborian battleship out here to make sure until you get back."

Ted nodded tersely. Terry turned to leave but stopped at the door of the CIC. "I don't know why, but I miss Ankh."

"I want my ship," Ted reiterated weakly.

"I know," Terry said, and walked face-first into Captain San Marino.

"I was looking for you," Micky said after bouncing back.

"Found me, you did," Terry said in his best Yoda imitation.

The skipper didn't know what to make of that, so he shook it off. "Rivka called. She needs our help. They're under fire."

"Do we have the coordinates?"

Micky nodded.

"Smedley! Battle stations. We've got to go save my lawyer!"

When Terry and an out-of-breath skipper arrived on the bridge, the Gate had already formed and was waiting for the order. Micky jumped into the captain's seat and ordered the ship through.

The *War Axe* appeared in the middle of a ragtag fleet of warships. The Magistrate's corvette was fighting and ducking, doing all it could to survive just one more moment.

"Fire the mains," Micky barked. On rapid fire at close range, it was like getting hit by so many nuclear weapons.

The enemy carrier shattered as if it were made of glass. Minor explosions disappeared quickly as the air became one with the vastness of space. Three frigates were vaporized before they realized a new enemy had appeared. Two more died when they turned to fight, and another died when it tried to run. The last one skipped off the upper atmosphere, using maximum acceleration to slingshot around the planet and head into deep space.

Without an on-board Gate drive, that ship was years from reappearing, if it reappeared at all. The physical Gate in the system would have to be monitored to prevent the pirate frigate from using it. Or Ankh and Ted could turn it off, only to be reactivated by use of a Federation code.

It would be years before any last holdouts from Mandolin reared their ugly heads.

"Nice shooting," Micky told his ship. "Get me that corvette, Smedley."

"My compliments on your timing, Captain," Rivka replied to the call.

Terry Henry pumped his fist. "Two wins in one day. You're going to spoil me, Skipper."

"Let's not do too much more of that." Micky's words were harsh, but he nodded and smiled.

"We've lost our Gate drive and one of our power supplies, and we left two people on the planet we need to pick up."

"Your final message has been transmitted." Erasmus' voice came over Rivka's open microphone.

"What? That was only if we died. We didn't die. You have to get it back!"

"No can do, Magistrate," the AI replied.

"Ankh!" she yelled.

"Do you need an escort to the planet's surface, Magistrate?"

"Oh, shit. You heard that? Never mind. Yes, we would like a ride if you can swing it. Open those big-ass doors of yours. Our ship needs a little work, and probably a new coat of paint, too."

Terry spoke loudly to make sure that Rivka could hear. "How is this lawyer thing working out for you, Barrister?" Char punched him in the arm.

"Ignore him," she told the Magistrate. "We appreciate the job you do. Micky's giving me the thumbs-up. The hangar bay is available. Please, relinquish thruster control to Smedley."

"What happened with the phantom destroyer and Keeg Station?" Rivka asked while docking procedures were underway.

"That's a story for a different day," Colonel Terry Henry Walton replied.

CHAPTER TWENTY-ONE

"Pod-doc!" Char declared, pointing at the hatch leading to the stairs that would take him to sickbay.

"We haven't even left orbit yet," Terry pleaded.

"This ship is plenty capable of leaving orbit and flying back to Keeg Station without the soon-to-have-his-ass-kicked Terry Henry Walton anywhere other than in the Pod-doc."

Cory leaned against the hatch's frame with her arms crossed, giving her father a heavy dose of stink eye.

"But..."

"But nothing." Char knew better than to try to drag him. "You promised. It's all over now, and you said you'd go into the Pod-doc and get checked out. Is your word going bad too?"

"My word is my bond," he deadpanned. "And there's nothing else going bad! Everything is working like it's supposed to."

"Then it'll be a quick trip to the doc, and you'll be back to your old self, getting in everyone's way."

"I don't get in anyone's way. I lead from the front," he declared.

"Yes, you get in people's way. They have this. Let the reconstruction and the healing begin, and Ted better figure out how that cloak works. Imagine if we had that for the *Axe?*"

"We should probably check on that—"

Char cut him off with a glance.

"After the Pod-doc, of course," Terry clarified.

He held his head high and strode briskly toward Cory, then started to run.

"Stop him!" Char shouted. Cory blocked the hatch with her body. Terry went to grab her and lift her out of the way, but Char was on his heels and rammed into him. Cory held tightly to one of his arms as he flailed to get free.

"You're going," Cory muttered with her head buried in his chest, hanging on for all she was worth.

Char had the other arm, and they frog-marched him up the stairs, not letting go.

He relaxed. "If anyone saw us, this would be embarrassing."

"You're worse than a little kid at bath time."

"Do I get to run naked through the corridors after it's over?" Terry asked.

"If you want, dear," Char said, her fingers white from maintaining a tight grip on Terry's arm.

"Eww!" Cory made a face but kept her hold. "Don't you dare."

When they reached the third deck, they found the corridor lined with friends, family, and warriors, who all started clapping.

"Son of a ..." Terry grumbled. He looked sideways at Char.

"Consider it leading from the front. If you're willing to get your centennial physical, then they will, too."

"Damn. This is what I get for marrying an older woman."

"Shh. Don't let those words ever escape your lips again," Char whispered.

"Going to get a recharge of the manly hydraulics?" someone quipped.

"What? Who said that?"

Snickers and shuffling answered his question.

"It's been nice knowing you, TH," Joseph shouted. Dokken barked, and a furry brown creature dashed through the group to bounce off Terry's leg, squeal in joy, and keep running as the German Shepherd bounded after her.

"Bye!" the group cried in unison.

Kimber jumped in his way and threw herself at him. "Don't leave us!" Terry pushed her back to find her laughing.

"With friends like you..." he started to say. He stopped and looked at those lining the corridor. "With friends like you, life is worth living. Let me get my nipple ring installed, then party on the mess deck! I hear there will be bistok," he shouted.

Cory and Char made eye contact. "Nipple ring?" Cory mouthed. Char winked in reply.

Terry stopped at the door of the medbay, but Ted waved impatiently. "Hurry up. I have stuff to do."

"Ted. I thought this was routine."

"Yours and Char's nanos are different from everyone else's, so they need an expert's touch. My alpha ordered me to do this, so I'm here. Don't make this any more painful than it already is."

"Painful? I'm sorry, Ted. What I meant to say was, 'I love you, man.'" Terry made big eyes, much to Ted's confusion.

Char pushed him toward the Pod-doc. Terry started dancing, slowly removing one piece of clothing at a time. Cory turned and motioned for people to go back into the corridor. "Show's over," she noted, closing and securing the hatch behind her.

Char crossed her arms and waited. Terry stopped dancing. "Fine."

He finished undressing and climbed in. The lid closed, and Ted went to work. He brought up the holomonitors and immersed himself fully as the programming on the nanocytes within Terry's body scrolled by. Ted tapped and worked, then sat down. The holoscreens disappeared.

"That's it?" Char wondered.

"That's it. Can I go now?"

"What was wrong with him?" Char blocked the door so Ted couldn't rush out.

"Some of the nanocytes, which should last forever, were worn out. Terry Henry Walton has worn out what shouldn't be capable of being worn out, but I chalk that up to the derivative nanos you two created. You are the only ones with this variety, although Cory's is a subset, different still from yours as well as everyone else's."

"Is he better?"

"His body is replicating replacements right now. That was all he needed. Oh, and as he gets older, if he wants to keep his mind sharp, he should take up crossword puzzles."

"Crossword puzzles?"

"Yes. I hear it's all the rage on Yollin to stave off dementia."

"I'll tell him, for what that'll be worth."

"He'll be done in two minutes. Can I go now?"

"Of course, Ted. And thank you."

She stepped aside so he could leave. Cory was waiting outside, arms crossed like a bodyguard.

"It'll be a while," Char shouted. "We'll meet you on the mess deck for a party. He's all right!"

The group cheered and stampeded for the stairwell. Cory made to enter medical, but Char stopped her, smiled, and closed the hatch.

"I know what you're doing in there!" Cory said to the closed door.

Char stripped, and when the lid on the Pod-doc opened, she climbed in and closed it behind her.

"Attention to orders!" Christina shouted. The Bad Company was already at attention, so no one moved. "Persons to be awarded, front and center."

Bundin and Bon Tap marched to the front of the formation, where Terry Henry Walton waited.

"There is much to be said for tradition, and one thing we don't do enough of is reward our people for superior performance in the face of danger. What we accept as commonplace, our everyday job, is anything but. We stand between life and death every single day. And sometimes, to complete the mission, we wrap death's shroud around us and claim the victory for all, knowing that we won't be there to celebrate in the end.

"Bundin did just that, demanding that we shoot the enemy beneath his feet since that was the only time we knew where it was. And Bon Tap, who defied orders to do the right thing by his squad leader. Together, they made it possible to destroy the enemy ship, and together, they made it out alive. It reinforces that we are better together than apart.

"For Bundin, a Silver Star. It's an Earth award, but nothing could be more appropriate for battles conducted in space. For risking his life to save the Gate, the station, and all of us. For Bon Tap, a Bronze Star for risking his life to save his squad leader. We have but one life to give, so let it be for something that matters—the defense of our fellows and the liberty we enjoy."

The *War Axe* hovered like a protective mother near her toddler. Keeg Station was setting a record on how quickly it could be rebuilt. Terry was trapped on the *War Axe*. His and Char's quarters had been destroyed, which didn't bother him at all, but the All Guns Blazing franchise had been gutted.

There was no beer, and they couldn't make any to replace what they'd lost because the tanks needed to be repaired. They also needed a new stock of hops and barley. It chapped his ass that the alien had cost him his escape from the rigors of running the Bad Company's Direct Action Branch.

He wanted to call Nathan and rag on him about something, but nothing came to mind. He settled for asking Christina to tell her dad that TH was mad at him.

For no reason whatsoever.

"We were supposed to be a private conflict-resolution organization." Terry rubbed his chin in thought. His and Char's quarters on board the *War Axe* were nice, almost a suite, and luxurious for a warship. But it was their home away from home.

"You know what?" Char purred. Terry stopped his meandering thoughts and gave her his full attention.

"There's a stock of beer in the galley's cooler."

Terry's face dropped. "You mean we've been sitting on beer all these weeks, and you've been holding out on me? You little vixen!"

"Had to wait until you were super-droopy. And for the record, you've been walking on it, not sitting." Char climbed into Terry's lap and wrapped her arms around his neck. "What about a vacation?"

"Not like that fifty years we did on Jamaica?"

"I had a great tan," Char countered. "But no. Just a week or two."

"It sounds like you already have something in mind." Terry put his arms around his favorite werewolf's waist and held her tightly.

"Pleasure moon around Cygnus VI."

Terry searched his memory. "A small planet on the frontier. Not a Federation member, but in good standing.

Supposed to have hot springs with healing minerals. Sounds like bromide-induced daze."

"Yes. It's perfect. We'll catch a ride on *Ramses' Chariot*."

"Ted is going to be on a pleasure moon with us?" Terry's sour expression made clear what he thought about that idea.

"No, but he and Felicity are taking a short trip to see their kids."

Terry relaxed. "There was a time not that long ago where a short trip wasn't ten thousand light years across the galaxy."

Terry coaxed Char from his lap and stood. "I heard there was a cold beer with my name on it."

"You can owe me..."

Terry turned back to his computer. "Holy shit!"

Char leaned toward him, wondering where her husband's mind had gone this time.

"I completely forgot about an RFP. I remember my last words when I looked at it were 'holy shit!'"

"Those are your words for just about everything." Char smirked. "Let me see it."

Terry moved aside.

"Holy shit!" Char exclaimed. She turned to TH and smiled. "Too bad you're going to put Christina in charge of it. We're going on vacation."

The End

I can't thank you enough for continuing to read this series. Terry Henry Walton and the fine characters who surround him have become a part of my world. I hope they've become a part of yours as well. Honor. Courage. Commitment. Things we can all live for and be proud of.

It has been eleven months since the last Bad Company. It was a business decision to move to a different series, and then a bunch of series, and then more stuff. But after nearly a year, it was time to return to TH, Char, and the good people who make the Bad Company what it is. Like old friends returning, once I started writing, it flowed like the old days. Maybe the break was good for me. I think this story is a unique take on the classics like *Run Silent, Run Deep* or even *Das Boot*—exceptional stories of leaders put into near-impossible situations, striving to best their opponent.

Talking about best, I'm teaching a class this session at the University of Alaska Fairbanks. They gave me a name badge and everything. The class is called, *How to Become a Successful Self-Published Author*. I have a non-fiction book by that name. I think I'm having more fun than my students. I love talking about self-publishing. They gave me a computer with the internet, and it projects onto the big screen. Dangerous, I know.

I try to keep the students engaged. I hope they're having fun. We'll see if I get lambasted in the course review. "Talks too much. One Star!" That's kind of funny—they don't do it that way there. I just won't be invited back.

The weather has turned uber-warm way early. We should have a full month of winter left, but spring has sprung. The snow is melting at the cyclic rate, and it's super slushy out there. Poor Phyllis the Arctic Dog has to get a full wipe down after being outside since it's muddy and nasty out there. At least it's warm. She likes it at 50F. Warmer than that and she pants like a big dog, which she is.

The warmth will also let us get into the woods behind our house that much sooner. Ten acres all to ourselves. That's hard to look at in the winter when we're blocked out by the snow. We couldn't keep a path clear this year, so no woods time for us. Soon, though. Phyllis can't wait to go in there and sniff the trees and moose tracks.

Back to the book. Nothing happens in a vacuum. I have a great number of people supporting me as I write. My insider team, the Skipper, Micky Cocker, Dr. Jim Caplan (Capples), Kelly O'Donnell, and John Ashmore gave me some in-process feedback. I gave them the first 25K words, and they gave it a quick read for me. They don't get the full story until after I get it back from my editor, Lynne Stiegler, and I hope they are pleased with the end result.

B'Ichi Aharche came from Bob Walters in our Kurtherian Gambit Fans and Authors Facebook group. I asked for names, and people came through! I asked for a man, woman, male, female, alien, and butthole. One can't have enough buttholes in one's back pocket, or maybe one is enough. Most importantly, I love that fans of these series are able to interact and help an author out.

Mandi Fawcett dropped some names, and Ruzfell caught my eye for the new systems specialist on board the *War Axe*. I thank you, Mandi for your contribution to the story. And to Heather Harris. I thought I could get away without having to name the weapons specialist, but then I couldn't, so I used the name you suggested – Katamara.

Sometimes one needs help in coming up with the appropriate insult, so I used the online Shakespearean Insult Generator for Joseph's comeback to TH.

Thou gorbellied dizzy-eyed pignut!

I had way too much fun clicking through the various insults. Shakespeare was the true master.

That's it—break's over, back to writing the next book. Peace, fellow humans.

Please join my Newsletter (www.craigmartelle.com – please, please, please sign up!), or you can follow me on Facebook since you'll get the same opportunity to pick up some of the books at fan pricing (only 99 cents) on that first day they are published.

If you liked this story, you might like some of my other books. You can join my mailing list by dropping by my website **www.craigmartelle.com** or if you have any comments, shoot me a note at craig@craigmartelle.com. I am always happy to hear from people who've read my work. I try to answer every email I receive.

If you liked the story, please write a short review for me on Amazon. I greatly appreciate any kind words; even one or two sentences go a long way. The number of reviews an ebook receives greatly improves how well it does on Amazon.

Amazon:
www.amazon.com/author/craigmartelle

Facebook:
www.facebook.com/authorcraigmartelle

BookBub:
https://www.bookbub.com/authors/craig-martelle

My web page:
www.craigmartelle.com

Thank you for joining me on this incredible journey.

THANK YOU for not only reading this story but these *Author Notes* as well.

(I think I've been good with always opening with "thank you." If not, I need to edit the other *Author Notes*!)

RANDOM (*sometimes*) THOUGHTS?

Old friends, new characters, and a galaxy we all visit from time to time…

There will be a special visitor in the next *Terry Henry Chronicles*… Some love her, some hate her, and some are just jealous of her shoe collection.

Some are afraid…very, very afraid.

There are a few Kurtherians out there focused on killing her. Here is a snippet from a future story where she is talked about…

UNEDITED

Uncharted Galaxy, Hidden Location

The Bitch. The Queen. The Empress.

Whatever she answered to, however primitive her beginnings, every remaining Kurtherian of the Seven clans knew her true name.

Death.

For two centuries now, Death had hunted them and harried them. With no rest or remorse, she had searched out the Seven and cut away their power, their resources, and their precious numbers. She had scattered them, driven them ever outward, and pursued them some more.

The absence of the Phraim-'Eh at this assembly was an affront.

There were no living Phraim-'Eh left to attend.

No longer a Prime, a Secondary, or a single Pilot among them, the remainder of the Seven clans gathered in the shadows of a cavern that did not belong to them. All of them hooded to conceal their identities, every Kurtherian present seethed in silence at being reduced to this deception by Death's ability to read minds.

Further, Gödel had culled those whose obsession with the moral high ground overrode their good sense to keep them all out of Death's crosshairs.

These were the survivors, the ones whose former quests for glory had been satisfied by smaller progressions along the path to Ascension. The ones who had been adaptable enough to recognize Gödel's greater wisdom and knew that all of their lives depended upon her leadership.

The silence grew in volume as many more joined the summit by mental link from their hiding places scattered across the galaxies—another precaution against total destruction should *she* find them. There were no snatches of conversation that might give away a connection. Even their exact numbers were hidden.

Gödel's law was simple to obey.

Give the humans *nothing*.

A low, reverberating chime sounded, signaling the arrival of the highest-ranking Kurtherian left alive to lead them. A solitary ball of Etheric energy came into being near the roof of the cavern, its pallid light casting the ancient carvings on the dais into relief—a reminder to the Azzhur present of the species they had wiped out when their clan took this planet centuries ago.

Gödel's entourage entered first. Two carried her throne onto the dais, and the other four fanned out at the base of the steps and raised their glowing hands to the roof. "Rejoice in supplication," they announced, "Gödel has come."

Every Kurtherian of the clans found the human cryptonym distasteful in the extreme. No one present knew their leader's true designation.

None dared ask.

Gödel exercised her skills with the Etheric with clinical abandon and pinpoint accuracy, as did her faithful. Meaning, she could call herself whatever she liked, and there wasn't a Kurtherian who had the power to question her.

The neutral silence took on an air of uncertainty as Gödel's guards mounted the dais and positioned themselves around the throne. Everyone was aware of how badly the summit would go if everything was not exactly how she expected it.

Gödel appeared upon the throne in a flash of light and a swirl of semi-diaphanous robes. The relief in the cavern was palpable when she settled back without passing comment—or killing them all in a fit of displeasure.

The absolute ruler of the Seven adjusted the fold of her ornate hood against her veil before folding her gloved hands in her lap. "Explain," she uttered in a dispassionate tone. "Explain to Us how Death, that irrational, emotional *human*, has managed to gain yet greater control over the Etheric."

A susurrus of denial echoed around the roof of the cavern.

Gödel lifted a finger, and a Kurtherian in the front row stepped forward. "Speak, T'sehmion. Tell Us and your brethren what you witnessed."

T'sehmion bowed their head and turned to the assembly. "Your Glory. My station was attacked by Death and her consort. They gave me no choice but to initiate self-destruct measures. All was lost, including the B'kheth."

Gödel's veil rippled as her mandibles jabbed at it. "How did she get past Our defenses?"

The red glow beneath the Kurtherian's hood dimmed as they turned back to Gödel. "I do not believe what I saw, your Glory."

Gödel leaned forward on her throne. "I see it in your mind, and it is the truth. Tell them." Her voice hardened, making her request a demand the Kurtherian dared not disobey.

T'sehmion bowed lower. "She walked out of an Etheric storm, but that isn't possible."

Gödel straightened, and the room flinched.

Her chin protruded beneath her veil, every word icy. "Nothing to say? Not *one* of you can hypothesize how she lived through it? How she walked into that storm and walked out at Our facility?"

No one spoke.

"Then what purpose do any of you *serve*?" Gödel demanded. "We were not ready for her to discover Our factories. If none of you can protect Our interests, then you are of no use to Us or to the future of the clans. We will replace you."

The room erupted into hushed whispers as Gödel got to her feet.

"We d-d-dare not m-move against her, your Glory," one of the hooded figures stuttered. "She is too p-powerful, and the revelation of her ability to ride the st-storm wall p-proves it without a doubt."

Gödel pointed a gloved finger around the room, smiling as she landed on the speaker and took control of his nanocytes. "We are *Kurtherians*," she calmly told the assembly as the speaker gasped his final breath. "Superior to all, submissive to none. We are the guardians of the path to Ascension, and we are at war.

She released the unfortunate to fall to the floor. "No longer can your duty be disrupted by the will of a single primitive female. You will all purge this blasphemous line of thought and find a way to rein in the humans, or it will be Our duty to cleanse our genetic pool of your weakness. There must be something we can use to remove Death from the equation."

Gödel glowed with absorbed energy. "Death desecrates our ancestors with her every breath, and it is all we can do to keep her distracted by continuous war. The years she vanished, we could find no trace of her. Now she is returned, stronger than ever and *We want her destroyed!*"

A curt voice broke the stillness of the cavern, taking the plunge for them all. "We are well aware of her weakness, Your Glory. However, unless we all have access to the knowledge you have gained…"

Gödel's laugh rang out across the cavern. "Have you begin to believe you can match Our Magnificence? We think not, Reben. It has become clear to Us, and to you, that the path to victory lies with Us, and Us alone. You are but weapons, and at the moment, ineffective ones at that."

The speaker's continued status as a living being encouraged another to speak up. "Your Glory, any move against the humans will result in disaster for us all. The charts—"

Everyone present suddenly found their ability to draw breath was no longer a given when Gödel lifted a hand and squeezed it into a fist. "We care not for the charts," she sneered. "We are *Gödel*. The prophecies are naught but amusements to those such as Us. We care only that Death and all of her allies are removed as an obstacle to Kurtherian dominion over all. This universe has a choice: obey Us and accept the gift of Ascension or die to bring that Age in."

Everyone in the cavern hitched a collective grateful gasp when Gödel dropped her grip on their airways and vanished.

Her voice echoed throughout the cavern—and their minds.

You will find a way to achieve it, or we will all die.

AROUND THE WORLD IN 80 DAYS

One of the interesting (at least to me) aspects of my life is the ability to work from anywhere and at any time. In the future, I hope to re-read my own *Author Notes* and remember my life as a diary entry.

I-15 Southbound heading to Stateline (couple miles north) going to LA

On my right side, outside the window are the mountains which rise up from the desert floor. The evening colors of the desert are splayed across the sky like a painting you might find in Sedona, Arizona.

In just a few moments, it will be dark here in the mountainous area as the sun drops below the horizon, and even the little bit of light outlining the mountains (hills?) around here will just fade into the night. The light will either be from the casinos we pass in Stateline or the ongoing line of white lights from cars coming from California to Nevada to try their hand back in Las Vegas.

Which, when I think about it, I want to encourage.

Would you fine folks from California *PLEASE* come to Vegas and continue to support our economy?

You would think that California, with its massive need for tax revenues, would recognize the huge opportunity to just allow gambling in zones inside California and keep the tax revenue.

I'm sure there are many and varied reasons why this won't work, and I'm too damned old to care to change anyone's opinion on the idea.

Besides, it puts money into the coffers of the city I live in, AND they gave us one of their football teams (Raiders).

Maybe we will leave things as they are and we all call it even-steven, California?

FAN PRICING

$0.99 Saturdays (new LMBPN stuff) and $0.99 Wednesday (both LMBPN books and friends of LMBPN books.) Get great stuff from us and others at tantalizing prices.

Go ahead. I bet you can't read just one.

Sign up here: http://lmbpn.com/email/.

HOW TO MARKET FOR BOOKS YOU LOVE

Review them so others have your thoughts, and tell friends and the dogs of your enemies (because who wants to talk to enemies?)... *Enough said ;-)*

Ad Aeternitatem,

Michael Anderle

Craig Martelle's other books (listed by series)

Terry Henry Walton Chronicles (co-written with Michael Anderle) – a post-apocalyptic paranormal adventure

Gateway to the Universe (co-written with Justin Sloan & Michael Anderle) – this book transitions the characters from the Terry Henry Walton Chronicles to The Bad Company

The Bad Company (co-written with Michael Anderle) – a military science fiction space opera

End Times Alaska (also available in audio) – a Permuted Press publication – a post-apocalyptic survivalist adventure

The Free Trader – a Young Adult Science Fiction Action Adventure

Cygnus Space Opera – A Young Adult Space Opera (set in the Free Trader universe)

Darklanding (co-written with Scott Moon) – a Space Western

Rick Banik – Spy & Terrorism Action Adventure

Become a Successful Indie Author – a non-fiction work

Enemy of my Enemy (co-written with Tim Marquitz) – a galactic alien military space opera

Superdreadnought (co-written with Tim Marquitz) – a military space opera

Metal Legion (co-written with Caleb Wachter) - a military space opera

End Days (co-written with E.E. Isherwood) – a post-apocalyptic adventure

Mystically Engineered (co-written with Valerie Emerson) – dragons in space

Monster Case Files (co-written with Kathryn Hearst) – a young-adult cozy mystery series

For a complete list of books from Craig, please see www. craigmartelle.com

www.ingramcontent.com/pod-product-compliance
Lightning Source LLC
Chambersburg PA
CBHW050248110726
47898CB00007B/2327